DOUBLE TROUBLE

Smile
Now.....
Die
Later!

"The vengeful cry of another ghetto tale!"

G. Prince 2014

www.ghettotheorywriting@yahoo.com
Copyrights: Ghetto Theory Publishing

ISBN 13-978-0-9897486-3-6

This novel is a work of pure fiction. Any names, characters, places and incidents are either the product of the author's imagination or are used fictitiously. Any resemblance to actual events or locales or persons, living or dead, is entirely coincidental. Any acts or performances by imaginary characters are the imagination of the author's visions, and not to be acquainted with any other persons, acts, or performances.

Synopsis

Kev Dog was a Pasadena Devil Lane who migrated to the streets of Denver Colorado to capitalize off the extreme benefits of the dope game. Jealousy turned to envy when rival gang members plotted to jack him for his money and dope, which ended in the death of him and his beloved fiancé. Kev Dog's greatest assist that he left behind was his twin daughters, Teyona and Keyona... who vowed to revenge their father's death, and go against one of the coldest kinpin's, and Crip gang leader to ever walk the ghetto streets of Denver Colorado.

His twin daughter's rage and hatred escalates into "Double Trouble" as they establish their own version of the ghetto art of war, which creates a vicious blood bath against the Crips and Bloods, leaving the innocence streets of Denver filled with body bags, twisted in a deadly ball of confusion.

This book is rated triple X for the extreme violent contents that has been realistically conveyed through the un-censorships that reflect the true urban struggles, and realities of the ghetto games.

Dedication

This book is first and foremost dedicated to the B's, C's, hustlers, players, gangsta's, and G's. Because the deepest part of the game, is understanding the real game, not the one that we learn to play, but the one that they used to play us!

"What happens when the predator becomes the prey, will the prey pray in the darkness of his cold cage that he will change his scandalous ways, and no longer be a slave to his ghetto characteristic traits?"

To my family.... I send my profound love! Also to Adaryll and Sheddrick White. I send a special shout out to you both, and I hope that, "at the feast, where all of the gangstas' and hustlers eat and meet, that you will be crowned best of the best, and may the jungle be conquered and placed at your feet.

Table of Contents

Chapter 1
Daddies Little Girls

It was the day of the Prom, and the twins Teyona and Keyona was all smiles and full of excitement, as they sat around the table of their plushed out four bedroom house, that was located in the out-skirts of Denver, Colorado. Part of their excitement was do to the fact that, their father Kevin Fox, better known as Kev-Dog by his street name, just told them that he would buy them both a brand new Cadillac Escalade truck, for their graduation present. Kev-Dog was at the dinning room table sacking up a kilo of powder cocaine, as he laughed and joked with his two beautiful daughters as he bathed in their joy.

A lot of people would frown upon the type of open relationship that Kev-Dog had with his two daughters, but he figured that kids growing up in society today, was a lot more faster now, then when he came up, and if anyone was going to lace his two daughters in the scandalous games of life, then it was going to be him! He was a street nigga, and the ghetto games was all that he knew.

Kev-Dog was a native of Pasadena California, where he was born and raised at, he was also a proud affiliate of the Pasadena Denver Lane Blood gang, that he wore proudly tattooed on his back. He did a five year bid in the

California State prison system, for a robbery that him and his ghetto love interest Ms. Lala, the twins now step mother, did together, and luckily she got away as he got caught and was sentenced to ten years.

However, being that it was his first real adult conviction, he only had to do half of his sentence before he was released on parole. Ms Lala was a true ghetto queen, and she rode the whole five year bid out with her man like a true thoroughbred. She was a stripper at the time when they met, and Kev- Dog's gangster suave character won her over, and she fell weak in her game of cat and mouse, and became the sucka to the game.

Ms Lala, was a beautiful light-skin sister with a body that would hypnotize a preacher, if he looked twice. And it was common for men to look twice as she walked by. Some people mistook her for Lisa Ray, because of her stagnating resemblance.

Kev-Dog on the other hand, looked like a ice cube type brother, with wavy hair that he wore in long French braid.

Teyona and Keyona were two of a kind. They both were real pretty brown skin girls with naturally wavy hair like their father. But, they got their pretty dark brown complexions and nice well built bodies, from their real mother who unfortunately got turned out on crack when they were five years old, and their father took custody of them. However, Teyona and Keyona looked like twin Ashanta's, and had the bodies to compare. Even though they were only 17 years old, they were truly wiser then their age, and Kev-Dog and Ms Lala made sure of this.

After Kev-Dog got out of prison on the robbery charge, he went and grabbed his twins up from his mothers house, went and got a fake ID and social security number, sold the diamonds that Ms Lala had stashed away and brought a new Chevy Tahoe truck, and three kilos of cocaine, and him, Ms Lala, and his twin daughters left California, and went and relocated to Denver Colorado, where the prices of cocaine was three times higher, and the niggas was a lot more greener.

It's been two years since Kev-Dog left California and re-established his game in Denver, and the money and game was sweeter then candy. He established a beauty salon called "True Beauty", for Lala and the twins, and a urban clothing store that sold all of the newest gear that hit the market, and his square ass cousin Robert moved down to clean up his life, so Kev-Dog let him manage the clothing store for him.

Life, or shall we say business, couldn't be better. Kev-Dog would go down to California every two months, and buy ten kilos for one-hundred and twenty thousand dollars, and bring them back to Denver and sale them ounce-for-ounce, for a thousand dollars a piece. Ounces was going for $1200 dollars a pop, so he would under cut his competition, and make three hundred and sixty thousand off of the ten birds. He would only sell the cocaine soft, because he knew that the Feds be fucking over niggas for selling it hard! His attorney put him up on the hundred to one ratio, for selling powder cocaine compare to cooking it up and selling it as crack. It was the difference between being white and black, and if he had to take a fall, then he knew that powder only carried ten years, compared to a life sentence for crack. So it wasn't hard to figure out what aspect of the game was best for him.

"So daddy tell me! Are you going to hook us up with some rims and sounds too?" Teyona said with her spoiled ass.

"Maybe!"

"Maybe what?" Teyona and Keyona said together, as if they had some sort of mind telepathy going on.

"Maybe is just a Maybe!" Kev-Dog joked, as him and Lala started busting up as they enjoyed the good high that the purple haze was giving them.

"See ya'll playin' and stuff...'Daddy!' Why are you playing with our emotions?" Keyona said.

* * * *

Even though Teyona and Keyona looked exactly alike, their characters defer in many ways. Teyona was the rowdy and aggressive one out of the two, and Keyona was more passive and considerate. Both was daddy's pride and joy, but Keyona compassion was the weakness in his heart and everybody knew it. Kev-Dog was a gangster by nature, so he taught his girls how to fight, talk shit, and shoot a gun, and they both was pretty good at it. Even Lala was required to carry a gun, but she did it with pride because she knew that her man was a gangster, and she was that unique reflection of his every desire for companionship. She loved the girls as her own, and they respected and loved her, the same.

"O'kay, check it out! If you promise to work at the beauty salon and clothing store for three months for minimum wage, then I'll do it."

"Damn daddy, we will starve to death off of minimum wage! Why you just can't let us deliver some sacks for you until we pay you back?" Teyona asked boldly.

"Because Tey, I already told you that I don't want you fuckin' with this shit! I take the risk so you won't have to. Now either you girls except my terms, or work and stack your own paper, and buy your own rims and sounds."

Teyona and Keyona rolled their eyes and pouted their pretty lips like young spoiled girls.

"Baby, why do you got to be so mean! It ain't nothing but some damn rims and sounds. Lala said in the girls defense. Come on baby, you know that you're girls deserve the best...quit being so hard on our babies!"

Teyona and Keyona gazed at each-other with a devilish smile, knowing that their daddy couldn't resist the compassionate pleads of all three of them.

"Yeah daddy please?" Keyona said.

"Yeah please daddy?" Teyona added.

Kev-Dog looked at Lala and then Teyona and Keyona and said, "Now that's fucked up....! Why can't I ever win when ya'll want something."

The girls laughed and jumped up and kissed him on the cheeks.

"Oh, now you'll happy again huh? Ya'll still going to work those three months at the shop... I'll pay you a little more, but don't be expecting no bank roll at the end of the week."

"Thank you daddy." The twins said in unison.

Kev-Dog shook his head as he reached over and grabbed his glass of Hennessy and took a big sip. "And another thang Lala, your fat ass is going to have to work extra too, since you want them to have some damn rims and sounds so bad!"

"O'kay baby, what ever you want me to do!" Lala said, as she gave him that sexy seductive look. And the girls smiled as they seen Lala hit him with that sexy charm.

"And don't be trying to use that little sexy seduction shit on me around my girls... you're going to make them think that I'm a sucka or something. What you trying to do, expose me or something?" Everybody started busting up as Kev-Dog made a silly grin...!

"Baby you know that I'll never do that, you're my handsome ghetto gangsta soulmate...and I love your dirty draws!" Lala stated as she lend over and gave him a kiss.

"That's crazy – for some reason I feel like a cold sucka... and love the feeling! Ya'll better learn from her, because she's one of the best."

The door bell rung....!

"I'll get it!" Lala said, as she got up from the table and went to go answer the door.

"Who is it?"

"UPS Maam, I got a package for a Kevin Fox."

Lala looked out of the peep hole and seen a young black man in a brown khaki suit, and a brown UPS hat and opened up the door.

As the door was opening the young man rushed in and pushed Lala back and grabbed her by the hair, as he pulled out a 9mm, and three other guys ran in behind him with ski masks on.

Lala screamed as the man struck her in the head with the gun, knocking her semi – unconscious.

Kev-Dog jumped up when he seen the three men rushing in, and Kev-Dog went for his gun that was in his belt behind his back, and the biggest mask gun-man shot him twice in the stomach with a 3.80 automatic and dropped Kev-Dog face down on the floor.

Teyona and Keyona screamed as they seen their father get shot, and they both dove on top of him as he hit the floor. Keyona was trying to shield Kev-Dog from anymore bullets, as Teyona was trying to go for her father's gun that was still stuck in his belt behind his back.

The gun man seen Keyona's reactions, and kicked her in the shoulder knocking her off of her father and away from the gun. Then he reached down and grabbed the gun and pocket it.

"Get that bitch!" The big gun man ordered as he pointed at Teyona. One of the other gun men grabbed Teyona by her hair, and drugged her over by the couch and put some plastic strip handcuffs on her, as the other gun man did Kev-Dog, Keyona, and Lala.

"Well, well, Kev-Dog – I've been waiting to catch you slipping for the longest. Ya'll don't stand around get the damn dope!" The big man said, as the other two robbers started gathering up all of the dope on the table.

"You!" The big man pointed at the robber who was next to Teyona, "go and search the bedrooms for the rest of the dope!"

The robber disappeared into the other rooms searching for the rest of the dope.

"Now Kev-Dog, you can save us some time, and you and your family some unnecessary pain, if you just tell us where the rest of the dope and money is!"

"There is no more dope and money here." Kev-Dog said, as his anger fought away the pain of his bullet wounds.

"Now come on? You don't expect me to believe that! You got a brand new 600 Benz and Vett parked out front, and we know that you've been pushing a lot of weight." The big man said, as he reached down and took off Kev-Dog diamond watch, rings, bracelet, and chain.

"You got everything, now just leave us alone… we won't call the cops." Lala said, as she laid on the floor handcuffed with the plastic restraints.

"Ms. Lala, the big man began, I've been fending for your sexy high yellow ass for awhile! Either you give us the rest of the dope and money, or we're going to be here partying until we find it." The big man said as he lifted up Lala's sun dress and said, "Damn, you know that I got to have some of this shit."

Lala, kicked at him as he slapped her and said, "Come and hold her wild ass down!"

"Man, we don't come here for that!" One of the masked robbers' said.

"Nigga I did… now somebody hold this bitch down! Listen bitch, either I'm going to fuck you, or I'm going to fuck one of them!" He gestured over toward the twins as Lala quit fighting back and just let him have his way.

"That's better." The big man said, as he pulled out his ten inch dick that was on rock hard, and ripped off Lala's panties and said, "damn your pussy's fat!" And rammed his dick all the way deep off into her womb.

Lala squalled in pain as the man said, "I know that you ain't had a dick this good!" As he humped his heart out.

"Get off of her you sick son-of-a-bitch!" Kev-Dog said, as he clinched his teeth trying to break the restraints.

"Shut up nigga, before I fuck you next… and make you my bitch! I know that your ass hole is tight!" He gave a little laugh as he felt his nut coming and started humping harder.

Lala felt her hand slip out of the restraints and when she knew that he was almost at his climax, she reached for his gun, and he seen her grab it, so he wrestled her holding her arm and hand as he yelled, "get this bitch!" And the other robber ran up and shot Lala in the face with a Snub Nose 44, and blow half her face off. Lala dropped the gun as she fell to the floor and he shot her in the chest.

"Nigga I told you that we didn't come here for that!" The gun men said, who was standing around watching.

"Fuck that shit nigga! I just spent a year in the pen, and I'm horny as hell. Now since that bitch didn't want to give me my nut like I asked her to, now I'm going to have to fuck one of these young hoe's, now you can watch, or go look for the damn money and dope, it's up to you." The big man said, as he stood their nursing his hard on.

"Man, just hurry the fuck up so we can get the fuck out of here."

"It shouldn't take long! I know that this young bitch got the fire." The big man said as he walked over to Keyona. Keyona started kicking at him. As he dove on her and started tugging at her shorts, as two of the robbers stood by and watched and laughed at the sick scene.

Teyona manage to slip her hands out of the restraints, and reached under the couch where her father kept his 357 magnum, then she came up busting. The first shot hit the robber who shot Lala in the face, dead off in his chest, and the hollo points knocked him against the wall as he dropped his gun on impact. The second shot hit the big man who was trying to rape Keyona, right in his forehead as he looked straight in her eyes as she pulled the trigger.

The third robber ran full speed as he jumped through the big glass window. Teyona shot twice but missed him. Teyona then jumped up to get the one who was still in the bedroom and as she glanced inside of the bedroom she saw that the window was opened, and she heard the car tires burn rubber as she glanced out of the window and saw two heads in an old black Regal leaving out the driveway.

Teyona ran back into the living-room and Keyona was kneeled over her father still in restraints. Teyona ran in the kitchen and got a knife, and ran back and cut the plastic restraints off her father and sisters hands. Then she knelt down next to her father.

"Daddy, daddy – don't die on us! The paramedic's will be here soon." Teyona uttered.

"Listen Teyona!" Her dad whispered as the girls bent down over his mouth. "Take care of each-other…! Remember what I taught you, and don't trust no-one. Go to the safe house and take the money and dope with you. Don't let the police find it, you hear..! The combination to the safe is 3 – 5 – 7. That's your money and dope now, so be smart, don't trust NO ONE! I love you both, watch your backs, and look out for each other o'kay?"

"O'kay daddy we will…. But you're going to make it!" Keyona said.

"Be strong babies and invest in businesses!" Kev-Dog died with those last words from his mouth.

"He's died Tey!"

"I know baby."

"Lala, Lala?" Teyona hollered.

Lala, opened up her right-eye that was left, and with her mouth which was half blown-off and she manage to ask, "is my man died?"

"Yes baby – Daddy's gone."

"I don't want to live like this – don't let me live like this." Lala uttered.

"Baby, it's not that bad... we can get it fix." Keyona said as she gazed into Lala's half blown off face.

"Please Teyona!"

Teyona got up and walked over and grabbed the robber's 44 magnum, and pushed Keyona out of the way and shot Lala in the heart.

"Teyona that was Lala!" Keyona yelled.

"Rest in peace Lala!" Teyona said. And walked over and unloaded the 44 magnum into the robber's face that shot Lala's face off. Then she turned and aimed the 357 magnum at the big man's crouch and empted the barrel, blowing his ten inch dick into tiny scattered pieces.

Keyona looked at the bodies in shock, as Teyona ran into the main bedroom and grabbed her father's brief case with the money in it, and said, "look Keyona! Look at me!"

Keyona looked at Teyona...

"Listen, take this dope and money and go to the safe house. I'll be there after the police leave."

"I can't leave you guys."

"Listen, Keyona – I ain't got time to argue with you right now. Take this shit and meet me at the safe house, and you don't know nothing! Do hear me?"

"Yes, but...?"

"No But...! Key, Key go so we won't go to jail."

"O'kay, O'kay, give me my keys! Are you going to be O'kay?"

"Yes, I'll see you as soon as I get rid of the police...stay there until I get there, and don't talk to no-one."

"O'kay, O'kay, I'm gone!" Keyona said, as she ran out and jumped into her fathers 600 Benz coup burning rubber out the driveway.

Teyona made sure that everything was straighten out before she called 911, and the police arrived on the scene ten minutes later.

Chapter 2
Tears Of Blood

"Hello Ms. Fox! Officer, take these damn handcuffs off her! I apologize for the inconvenience Maam. My name is Detective Smith, and I'm the homicide Detective who has been assigned to this case. This here is Detective Jones from our drug division."

Teyona looked over at Detective Jones, and recognized him from around the neighborhood that she grew-up around. Detective Jones was well known and had a big reputation for busting a lot of the drug dealers around the city.

"Ms. Fox, please except our condolences." Detective Smith said as he continued to speak. "I know that this must be a very complicated situation for you to deal with, but I must ask you some questions, so we can fully understand what transpired here. Now you spoke briefly with one of the officer's, and he gave us a brief explanation of what you said happened. But can I get you to please reiterate the situation for us, so we can try to understand it better?"

Teyona shook her head "yes", as she wiped a tear from her tear stained cheeks and said, "well me and my family was sitting at the dining room table, when someone knocked on the door. My step-mother went to answer it, and four men with guns and ski mask came running in. When my father seen them he jumped up from the table and the big man over there, 'and she gestured toward the dead man', he shot my father twice in the stomach, and then they started handcuffing everybody with those plastic restraints.

The big man was asking my father to give him some money, and my father told them that he didn't have a lot of money here. Then the big man said that he knew that my father owned some businesses, so he had to have some money stashed around here some-where. My father told him that all his money was in the bank, and if he wanted, he would go withdraw him whatever he wanted, just don't hurt us. The big man didn't believe him, and told the other men to search the house.

Then he went over and started raping my step-mother. My step mother must have got out of the hand restraints while he was raping her, because they started wrestling for his gun, and then the other robber ran over and shot my step-mother in the face. 'And Teyona paused and wiped another tear from her eyes, as she stared at the floor for a brief moment' and said, "then he shot her twice in the chest and killed her!"

Teyona looked at the Detective in the eyes and said,
"They just killed her like it wasn't anything." Then she
wiped her eyes as the Detective gave her his handkerchief.
Teyona wiped her eyes and nose and said, "then one of the
robbers started arguing with the big man, and told him
that he didn't come here for all that crazy shit, and kicked
him in the dick, and the big man fell to the floor on his
knees holding his balls'.

At that time, I was able to get my hands out of my
restraints, and remembered that my father kept a gun
under the couch, so I grabbed the gun, and shot the first
man, who shot my step-mother in the face, and he fell
against the wall over there," and Teyona gestured toward
the gun man who was dead against the wall.

"Then I shot the big man as he was holding his balls'
on the floor, he was on his hands and knees, and when he
looked at me, I shot him dead between the eyes.

The other robber ran and jumped out of the window.
I shot at him and missed him, so I ran into the bedroom to
get the one who was in there searching, and when I got
there the window was open and he was gone. I looked out
of the window and seen two heads in a green Regal
speeding away. I ran back in the other room and saw that
my father and step-mother was dead, so I grabbed the big

man's gun and shot him in the face again and in his dick
for raping my step-mother." And both the Detectives
spontaneously grabbed their dicks, at the thought of being
shot in the dick.

"Did the robber say anything about any drugs"
Detective Jones asked?

Teyona looked at him and said, "nope, not that I
heard."

"Ms. Fox, is it anything else that you can remember
about the other two robbers that can help us identify them.
Any names, tattoos, size, handicaps, or anything at all?

"No sir, not that I could remember!"

"And they never mentioned anything about any drugs
or anything" Detective Jones repeated?

"No sir, I would have remembered something like
that!"

Detective Smith looked at Detective Jones and said,
"well Ms. Fox, I'm going to leave you my card just incase
you remember anything. I'm going to consider them
murders in self defense, because you had every right to do
what you did to protect yourself from them sick sons-of-
bitches. As soon as we find the other two assailants, then I
guarantee you, that they will pay way worse then there
buddies over there. Now, will you be alright?"

Teyona watched the Coroner as they carried her father
out in a body bag. Then she wiped her eyes and shook her
head and said, "Do I have no choice."

"Do you have a place to stay for a couple of days? It's
best for you not to stay here!"

"Yes, I'll go stay with my auntie!"

"O'kay, we will be here doing our little investigation
well into the night, but we will have someone come and
board up this window before we leave. If you want to
grab something's before you leave, then this officer will
assist you," and Teyona turned around and seen the
female officer standing in back of her, "also she would
need some information from you and will provide you
with all of the information that you need to know about
your father's and step-mother's where-about's, so you can
provide them with the proper burial arrangements. Again
Maam, I am so sorry that you had to go through this tragic
ordeal, and if it's anything that I can do, or you hear
anything that might help us in our investigation, then
please don't hesitate to call me. O'kay!"

Teyona shook her head as she watched the Coroner
carry Lala's body bag to their truck.

Detective Jones said, "Don't you have a twin sister?"

Teyona looked at him with a hidden surprise look on her face and said, "Yes, she's at my auntie's house.

"Will she be o'kay?"

"I hope so – today was our Prom night, so I can imagine how much this will destroy her. Hopefully, we can find away to live on." And a tear dropped from Teyona's eyes but it wasn't from the pain that she felt anymore, those tears was all cried out. This tear now was from the hatred that was strongly building up in her empty heart, and the only feelings that she embraced was that of vengeance."

Teyona grab a suitcase and throw some clothes and personal valuables for herself and her sister, and jumped into her father's new convertible Vett, and sped away in the dark, leaving this nightmare that she just went through behind her.

"What do you think?" Detective Smith asked.

"She's lying! This was clearly a drug related jack move gone bad! Her father was in the game knee deep. We've been after him for the longest, but he was pretty clever. He only sold powder cocaine and didn't trust too many people. I'm surprised that anyone even found out where he laid his head at! We had an informer on him once, but our informer mysteriously came up dead in

Texas. Also, word has it that, he was the one who shot Big Al's lieutenant at the club around eight months ago, you remember when Paper got shot at the club."

"Oh yeah, I remember it now!"

"Yeah, Mr. Kev Dog was a true gangster, but like all dope dealers, they don't seem to last long!" Detective Jones agreed as Detective Smith just shook his head.

"Well keep your ears to the ground on this one. I want to know who's responsible for this sick shit, and I want the other two assailants on death row. We're not going to tolerate this type of crazy shit out here in my damn town! Do I make myself clear on that Detective?"

"Yes Sir. Lieutenant Smith." Detective Jones said as he left out.

Chapter 3
From The Cradle to the Grave

Keyona was looking out of the window of her father's stash spot house, which was in a nice quiet community in Denver suburbs, and seen Teyona getting out of her father's new convertible Vett with a suit case. Keyona let out a loud breathe as she ran and opened up the front door for her sister.

Teyona seen Keyona open up the front door and a painful expression of relief was on her face. Teyona walked in the door and put down the suit case, as Keyona turned the lock on the door, and gave her big sister a big hug, and then started crying in Teyona's arms. Teyona anger wouldn't let her cry no more, but she held her sister in her arms and rubbed her back, as Keyona let out her agony.

"It would be alright Key, Key! Go ahead and let it all out baby." Teyona said, as she walked Keyona over to the couch and cuddled her in her arms.

"Tey, Tey they killed daddy and Lala for nothing…they just murdered them in cold blood! What kind of person would do something like that?"

Teyona said, they we're demons Key, Key and we're going to hunt them dirty sons-of-bitches down, and send them back to hell were they belong!"

"Tey, Tey let's just leave! We can sale the businesses and take the money and start a new life back in California with grandma."

"Key, Key, I don't want to hear that scary weak shit from you...! Those niggas just killed our father and step-mother in cold blood, and I wouldn't be able to live my life no where, without making those niggas pay! My father wouldn't be able to rest in peace with these sons-of-bitches still breathing."

"Let the police take care of them.....that's what they do."

"Fuck the police Key, Key! This is my fight, if you want to take the money and run, then you take your scary ass on and do so. But, I'm going to make them niggas pay for what they did to my family, with you or without you. I don't need you with me anyway if you're not total down with me." Teyona pushed Keyona off of her, and got up with fire in her eyes as she walked into the bedroom.

Teyona knew how to persuade her sister to do anything, but she had to show Keyona some rejection and act like she was mad at her for Keyona to break down and submit. They were twins, so rejection and separation was as painful as the thought of losing one another. Keyona didn't ever want to bare that pain.

"O'kay, Tey, Tey, "Keyona said, as she wiped her eyes and walked into the bedroom where Teyona had open-up the safe.

"O'kay What?" Teyona said in a mad voice!

"O'kay I'm down with you!"

"You ain't got to be down, you can leave and take the money and run if you're scared." Teyona opened the door to her father's big safe that he had built into the wall closet of his master bedroom, as they looked both of their eyes got big, then Keyona said, "Damn, how much money do you think that is?'

"I don't know, but it looks like a lot." Teyona said.

"Come on help me count it!"

They both took hands full of money that was in stacks, and walked over to the bed and started counting it.

Two and a half hours later Keyona said, "I got $296,000 thousand over here!" And Teyona said, "I'm almost finished. Go and get the brief case that you took from the other house and count that too."

Keyona ran in the other room to retrieve the brief case, and then open it and started counting the money that was stacked up in that.

Fifteen minutes later, Keyona said, "its $36,000 dollars more. That makes this total $332,000 dollars."

"I got $356,000 thousand over here, which makes it all a total of $688,000 thousand dollars." They both said together as they stirred at each other in disbelief.

"We're rich Tey, Tey!"

Teyona opened up a big legal envelope that had some documents in it, she pulled them out and started reading them. "This is the deeds to this house and the other house. These other papers are the lease and business licenses to the beauty salon, and clothing store. They're all in our name."

"Look Teyona, what's that?"

Teyona picked up a small plan white envelope that was sealed she opened it and inside was a letter.

"It's a letter from daddy!" Teyona said.

"What do it say, Tey, Tey?"

"Dear Keyona and Teyona,

How's my two princesses doing? I hope and pray being strong like I always taught you to be.

If you are reading this letter, then the game lord has chosen to take me out of the game. It's nothing for you to be sad about, because I was a all star player, and as you can tell, the game was good.

Everything that I own is yours now! My attorney's name is Robert Parker, and he will give you another envelope that I put up for you. He's a very good and true friend, and if you ever get into trouble, then call on him, he will be there for you always.

I urge you both to not get involved in the game. Go further your education and invest in businesses. You both are very smart, and have a lot to offer the world... so play your part.

I expect you two to always watch over each-other, and never turn you're back on one another, and never let nothing or no one come between you two. You two was born together, so god planned for you both to stick together in life – for life!

Don't trust anyone outside of yourselves, and take care of grandma and Lala! Lala loves you both like her own, so be good to her, because she would die for you both.

The other stuff that's left behind, if you don't know what to do with it, then find a good cause and donate it. Because the game must go on!

Love could never define the emotions that I feel for you, so don't ever question what we will always possess. We are spiritual soul-mates forever, so please don't ever think that I'm not with you, because we will be as one for eternity.

"Live like princesses, and rule like queens, and never forget were you come from."

Thanks for allowing me to know true love!

Eternally Yours, Daddy!

Aka "Kev Dog."

P.D.L. 4 Life!

"Tey, Tey, he knew that he would die soon. It's like he was preparing us for when he left so we wouldn't ever want or need for anything while he was gone."

Teyona felt the same way, but she couldn't let her sister know it, so she played it off and said, "Listen Key, Key, you can take the damn money, and go start you a new life in California or the damn Bahamas! I don't care! I'm going to revenge my father's death with you, or without you."

35

"Tey, Tey, I'm down with you! Daddy wouldn't ever forgive me if I left you hanging. Plus, I'm a better shot then you!" Keyona said, as they both broke into a smile.

"But first let's bury our love ones, and get our business affairs taken care of before we do it, because afterwards, we're getting the hell out of this place! Deal..!"

"Deal, but I'm not going to be waiting no long time! After the funeral it's on, whether you got everything together or not."

"You're so fuck'in stubborn Tey, Tey!"

"So what... I'm a gangsta bitch! Ain't nobody going to kill up my whole family and I just except that shit. You got to be going crazy!"

"Fuck it Tey, Tey....whatever happens, just happens, but let's make sure that we buy some extra grave sights next to daddy and Lala, because we might be visiting them sooner then we plan!"

"Don't worry sis, we're going to do it right. We got to much to live for now, so don't think that we're going to just be no fools about it. We're going to be smart, plan, and cover our tracks, and then we're out!"

Keyona just looked at her sister and shook her head, she seen that conniving look before, and knew that it meant nothing but problems, and troubles.

* * * *

The next day Keyona and Teyona made all of the necessary funeral arrangements, and called all of the family members and informed them of the tragic ordeal. Keyona dropped a tear as she heard her grandmother break down over the phone.

"My baby, My baby, My baby, why Keyona?

"I don't know grand Ma!"

"Who did it?"

"We don't know grandma."

"Find out for me Key, Key – I want them to pay for this, you hear me? They're going to pay for killing my baby!"

"I hear you grandma."

"You need money? I got some money for you!"

"We're fine grandma! We just made the funeral arrangements, and the funeral would be held in a couple of days on Saturday. So why don't you get a fight out here and you can stay with us so we can put daddy and Lala to rest together?"

"Okay baby, I'll pack my clothes and book me a flight for tomorrow. Are you sure that you girls don't need no money?"

"No grandma, we're fine…. Daddy left us some."

"O'kay don't worry, grandma will be there tomorrow baby. I'll call you and let you know when my flight lands."

"O'kay grandma, talk to you then!"

"O'Kay baby, bye!"

"Bye."

Keyona let out a deep breath as she hung up the phone. Kev Dog's Mother, Fay was a down gangster girl back in her younger years too. She sold dope before, and drove in some robberies with her ex-boyfriends. And even did a couple of drive byes with one of her old ex-boyfriend who was a cold gang banger from the Notorious East Coast Crips, out of South Central L.A. But that was way back in the day. Kevin was just a little snotty nose kid at the time, and his grandmother was keeping him while Fay ran the streets. Fay's mother died when she was 21 years old, and Kevin was 5, so Fay slowed down on the gangster stuff, and just hustled a little to make ends meet. The little money that she made by selling crack in the Kings Manner Projects in Pasadena were she migrated to from L.A., was good money considering that she was on welfare and was receiving housing assistance. So she was very familiar with the street games, and was as down as they came.

Kevin started hustling in the projects at 13 years old. He did a 4 year bid in youth authority when he turned 14 years old and got out when he was 18, he had become a true bonafide gangster. Fay stuck by his side and kept his books fat, and even took him some weed every blue moon, so he could make some extra money while he was down. Their relationship was more like sister and brother, instead of mother and son. Kevin was her pride and joy! When Kevin got caught up on the jewelry store robbery, Keyona and Teyona stayed with Fay, and Lala would come and get them and take them to see their father at Lancaster State Prison, sometime they all would go. Fay loved Lala like a daughter, because Lala was down for her son and a young gangsta bitch too. Fay and Lala were like sister's, and now her worse nightmare had come true and only blood could stop pain that weighed so heavily in her heart.

* * * *

Keyona went into the bedroom where Teyona had found the guns hidden away in her father's closet, and next to the guns laying on the bed was four whole kilo's of cocaine, the other kilo that her father was sacking up right before them nigga's ran in and killed him.

"I just got off the phone with grandma" Keyona said.

"Is she o'kay?" Teyona said, as she looked up at her.

"I don't know – you know how grandma is!"

Teyona smiled at the thought. "Exactly." Keyona said, "and she'll be on the next flight out here, in the morning."

"Good...what did she say?"

"Basically, the same thing that you said! Find them nigga's that did this to my son and Lala, and kill them all!"

"That's my girl.... I knew that grandma was going to want to ride."

"Yeah, you two is just like one another." And they both laughed.

"Keyona picked up the Mac 10 and cocked it, and reflected back on when her father was teaching her how to shoot.

"Now Key, Key, don't be scared of it, you're in control, and you tell it what to do! Now hold it steady at about stomach height, and put this hand on top of here so you can easily handle it and control it. Hold your breath and shoot." Then Keyona let off a round and it felt easy for her, so she let off another two rounds. Keyona looked up at her daddy and smiled then she said, "I like this one!"

"O'kay, there are three more fifty round magazines.... Practice with them and remember you want only three to four bullets to come out at a time, so concentrate Key, Key and don't close your eyes, it won't hurt you."

"O'kay daddy."

Keyona smiled at the memory and seen Teyona holding up her pride and joy, the modified 12 gauge Moosebird automatic pump with the pistol grip, and shook her head as Teyona looked at her and smiled.

"Here Keyona, keep this 3.80 on you at all times...no telling if those niggas will try to come back and kill us. Now go get dress, we got to go stop by the beauty salon and clothing store, and make sure that Kim and cousin Fred know that we expect them to keep the operations going professionally, while we're taking care of our family business. As long as they know that we're on them, then we shouldn't have a problem with our management. We gotta go and pick out the flower arrangement."

Teyona put up the dope and wiped the guns, and put them back in there stash spot, and put the 21 shot Gloc 9mm in her purse, as she got dressed, then her and Keyona jumped in the Vett to attend to their family business.

Chapter 4
A Woman's Scorn X2

After the twins got through attending to their family business they we're stopped at a red light on the corner of Colfax and Broadway, when Teddy from a blood set called Crenshaw mafia out of Denver pulled up on the girls and said, "hey Teyona, what's up girl?"

Teyona grabbed her gloc that was on her lap as she looked over at the older heavy set brother in the Lexus 400.

"Do I know you?" Teyona asked as Keyona eased her hand into her purse grabbing the butt to her 3.80.

"Yeah Boo – me and you're dad was real cool..! That was my relative. Listen, I know about what happen and my condolences to you and your sister, but if you're interested in knowing who else was involved, then follow me."

Teddy pulled off as the light turned green, and Teyona looked over at Keyona and started following Teddy as Teddy pulled into the Mc Donald parking lot and parked. Teyona looked at Keyona and said, "Stay on point," as she pulled up and parked next to him, and she and Keyona both jumped out with their hands in their purses.

Double Trouble

Teddy got out of his Lexus smoking a new port and seen the twins getting out of the Vett with their hands tucked into their purses, he said, "slow down little ladies – I come in peace!"

"You know who killed my father?" Teyona asked.

"Yeah Boo! My girl got a home-girl that fucks with one of Big Al's lieutenant's that nigga Paper, and Paper ran his mouth to her and said that Little Sam, and Tate was the one's who got away. The other two didn't make it out! Your dad use to show me a lot of love, and I'm not feeling that shit that happened. Kev Dog, was a Domu so he was my relative also. So, if it's anything that I can do, then holla at me."

"You want to make a bird?" Teyona asked.

"Hell yeah – what's up?"

"I want you to contract one of them and tell them that you're trying to cop a couple of ounces. Have him meet you at the motel, and me and my sister will deal with him from there."

"That's what's happenin' – you damn right I'ma call that nigga. As a matter of fact, I got his number in my car. I'll call that nigga on my cell right now and see if we can get him to bite.

Teyona gave a vague smile that Keyona caught,
and know what she was thinking.

* * * *

Teddy got in contact with Tate, and Tate agreed to
meet Teddy at the Travel Lodge on Colorado to sell him a
couple of ounces. Teyona stopped at the hardware store
and then jumped back in her Vett and parked around the
corner. Then she jumped into Teddy's Lexus as Teddy
went to rent the room in an alias name, then he and the
girls walked into the motel room.

"What do you got in the bag Teyona?" Teddy asked.

"Just some goodies for our little party."

Teyona, started laughing as Teddy smiled and Keyona
just shook her head, because she know what her sister was
about to do.

Five minutes later Tate drove into the motel parking
lot and parked his new Dodge Magnum wagon next to
Teddy's Lexus. Teddy saw him drive up so he opened the
door to the motel room and waved him in.

Tate walked in and shut the door and said, "What's
up Teddy, I didn't think that you would ever get in touch
with me!"

"You know how it is man, my last connection just got taken-out of the game, so I got to try to find a new source."

"Hey you know how that go's, nigga's fall victim to the game everyday." Tate said as he gave a small laugh.

"They sure do!" Teyona said as she came out of the bathroom with her gun drown and pointed at Tate's head.

"Oh shit! What's up man?" Tate asked, as Teddy socked him in the jaw and sent him flying to the floor.

"That's what's up nigga," said Teddy.

Tate was on the floor half unconscious as Teddy took Tate's 38 revolver from his belt.

Teyona went into her paper bag and pulled out some plastic restraints, then throw them to Teddy and said, "tie that nigga up for me."

"I got you Tey, blood put your damn hands behind your back, before I beat shit down your muthafucken leg."

"Och, och, O'kay man, why ya'll trippin?"

"Shut up nigga!" Teddy put the restraints on Tate, and flipped him over. "There ya'll go Tey."

"So Tate, long time no see!" Teyona begin as Keyona went and sat at the table across for Teddy.

"Why ya'll trippin' on me? I ain't did nothing to you." Said Tate as he watched Teyona reach into the paper bag and put on some brown gloves, his eyes got big as he looked across the room at Teddy setting at the table.

Teddy shook his head, "you fucked up blood – maybe you should tell the truth and you might not get yourself killed today," said Teddy laughing.

Tate looked back at Teyona as she putted out a hammer, some big nails, a screwdriver, and some pliers and spread them out on top of the dresser.

"Wait a minute girl – that's not necessary! I'll tell you what you want to know, just don't kill me," Tate said as he was squirming on the floor, ready to shit in his pants.

"O'kay who sent ya'll to come and rob my father?"

"It was Big Al..! He said that your daddy was taking up too much of his territory and money, so he sent us and Big C. to rob ya'll. We was just suppose to rob you, but Big C. started trippin out with that rape shit. 'you heard me tell him that we didn't come there for that – didn't you'?"

"Who else was with you that jumped out of the window?"

"That was Little Sam – you smoked Big C. and Bird."

"How much did Big Al pay you?"

"He had Paper give me and Little Sam a bird a piece, but you can have it all, I didn't want it to go down like that, all that shit was uncalled for, and I'm sorry that it happened."

"You're sorry huh..!"

"Yeah and if you let me go, I promise I won't tell a soul...I'll leave town just please don't kill me."

"Where do Big Al and Paper live at?"

"I don't know – I think that they got a spot in Westminster somewhere. I can probably find out and let you know!"

"What about Little Sam?"

"He be over there on Lake and Laurence. He got a spot there and he be serving on Colfax."

"Damn the nigga's telling his ass off, boy I'd hate to be your crimee you'd tell it all and get everyone killed," Teddy said as he started busting-up laughing.

Teyona went into the bathroom and came out with a face towel, she said, "Here suck on this bustard, maybe it won't hurt as bad." Then she balled the towel up and tried stuffing it in his mouth.

That's – fuck – up – bitch, Tate was tossing his head from side to side cursing. Then Keyona got up and kicked him in his balls, as Tate open his mouth hollering in pain and Teyona stuffed the towel down his throat.

"Thanks Key, Key!" Teyona said as she giggled and Keyona smiled.

Teyona grabbed the hammer and swing it as hard as she could hitting him on his right knee, and broke it.

"Damn that had to hurt!" Teddy said as he laughed and took out a cigarette and lit it up.

Tate screamed a muffle sound as Teyona swung the hammer again hitting him in the left knee, cracking it intensely. That was it, the pain was so severe that Tate started shitting in his pants and peeing all over his self.

"Keyona…!" – Teyona said as she looked at her sister and said, "come-on, finish him off."

"NO, Teyona go ahead – I'm cool..!"

"What-ch' you mean you're cool?"

"This is the same son-of-a-bitch that killed our father…! He shot daddy and Lala in cold blood, and was going to rape you and me and kill us both…! And now he's bagging for mercy and you say "NO!" Get your ass over here avenge our father death!"

Keyona looked at Teyona and then at Tate on the floor with tears in his eyes, then over at Teddy who was still setting at the table smoking a cigarette. Teddy said, "fuck it girl – that nigga's murdered your family in a cold blood – fuck that nigga up!"

48

Keyona slowly got up and walked over to the dresser and picked up the big screwdriver that was lying there, then she looked back at Teyona and Teyona said, "he killed our daddy Key, Key – Kill that son-of-a-bitch for us, avenge our family!"

Keyona walked over to Tate and looked down at him, then she jumped on top of him and started stabbing him in his chest with all her might, driving the screwdriver straight through like a spear, then looking him in the eyes, plunged the screwdriver straight through his eye socket. Keyona got up and was covered with blood, and Teyona took the hammer and hit the top of the screwdriver and made it shoot out the back of his head. His body shook uncontrollable as his blood poured out of his dead body.

"Go get cleaned up Key, Key and don't leave no fingerprints." Teyona said; as Keyona stood there looking at the blood on her hands then she walked into the bathroom to wash it off.

"Ya'll some gangsta bitches for real! That's the type of shit I need in my life. I'll leave my baby's momma and my mistress for your young fine ass." Teddy said with a grin.

"Yeah right nigga – help me wrap this nigga up in that quilt."

They put Tate body on the bed and Teddy said, "wait..! Take off Tate's diamond ring, chain, and gold watch. And get his money and dope out of his pocket; "NOW…!"

They rolled Tate up in the quilt as Keyona walked in with a wet towel, wiping the blood off of her self.

"Come on, help me take him into the bathroom and put his shitty ass in the tub."

Teddy grabbed the quilt and said, "Let me just drag his stinky ass." And he started pulling him into the bathroom.

Teyona followed him into the bathroom and Teddy looked up and said, "What's the pillow for?" then three muffle shots went off as Teddy looked down at his shirt and saw the blood from the three bullet holes and, before he fall down he said, "Damn girl, that's fucked up." Then Teyona shot two more times and blow his brains out of the back of his head and all over the wall.

Keyona ran into the bathroom and seen Teddy dead laying over the quilt that Tate was rapped up in and seen the Gloc 9mm in Teyona's hand and screamed, "why did you have to kill him Tey, Tey?"

"Because he knew to damn much! You know that we can't trust that nigga, you remember what daddy said! If

50

he would set Tate up for a kilo, then he would set us up for a key too! Now go and get them other gloves and put them on and get the liquid acid out of the bag for me." Teyona waited until Keyona got back, and they picked Tate and Teddy up, and throw them in the bath tub. Teyona pulled the screwdriver out of Tate's eye and part of his brains and eye ball was attached to it.

"Uuuug!" Keyona said, "I don't like looking at that!"

"You did it…!" Key, Key don't start getting all yucky on me now," said Teyona. "Grab a towel and start wiping down the motel room for me. Try to remember everything that we might have touched, and wipe it down too, so that we don't leave any prints."

"O'kay," Keyona said; as she grabbed a towel and left out.

Teyona poured the acid on Teddy and Tate's face and hands, then wiped down the bathroom sink area and poured the rest of the acid over the sink just incase Keyona left some of her DNA behind while she was washing up. Then Tey, wiped down all of her tools and left out. She took Teddy's Lexus as they drove around the corner and parked. Then she wiped it down and jumped back into their father's Vett, and separated the tools one-by-one as they disposed of everything.

* * * *

The twins made it back at their stash house by nine o'clock that evening. They decided to take a shower and changed their clothes, when they were finished, Teyona went and throw all their clothes into the washer machine and added a gang of bleach. The bleach washed the color out of everything, but that was what Teyona wanted. Then she put the clothes into a large plastic trash bag, and drove to the supermarket. When she got there she circled around the back of the store, and grabbed the trash bag that was in the back seat of her car that had the bleach clothes inside, then she jump out of her car and grabbed the bag and threw it, into a big trash dumpster that was in the alley. Then Teyona drove back around to the front of the store and parked the car and went in. Inside the supermarket she grabbed some food for them to put inside the refrigerator.

When she got back home she found Keyona sitting in the bedroom watching TV with no sound on, listening to Tupac CD that was playing through the stereo system at a soft mellow tone.

"Now that's that gangsta shit that I like – do you want some ice cream? I got your favorite kind, Butter Pecan!"

"Yes, I'll take some."

"How about I just go grab two spoons and we share it with these Famous Amos chocolate chip pecan cookies." She said, as she smiled at her sister and went to grab the spoons.

Teyona walked back into the bedroom with the two spoons and they sat on the bed and shared the ice cream and cookies like they use to do as little girls.

"Tey, Tey, I can't lie… It kind of felt good to kill them son-of-bitch that killed our father and Lala."

"I know baby, it felt good to me too! They took all that we ever loved like it wasn't nothing. Don't get me wrong, I don't want to become a cold blooded killer! But, I can assure you, that everybody who had a hand in our father and Lala death will die before I give up. We just got to be smart and cover up our tracks, and when we finish then, we're out of here."

"Hopefully!" Keyona said as she looked at her sister with that I hope that you're right look.

"Listen, we got to go see daddy's attorney tomorrow and pick up grandma at the airport, so we better try to get some sleep."

"O'kay." Keyona said, as they cut off the light and both cuddled up like little girls and went to sleep.

Chapter 5
Momma's Heart and Soul Bleeds Revenge

The following morning Teyona and Keyona got up early to meet there 8:00 o'clock appointment with their father's attorney.

"Excuse me Maam, my name is Ms. Fox, and I have an 8:00 o'clock appointment to see Mr. Parker."

"Yes, Ms. Fox – Mr. Parker has been expecting you." His secretary said, "Just one moment please." The secretary got on the phone and said, "Mr. Parker … your 8:00 o'clock appointment is here. Yes sir!"

"Please follow me ladies." As the secretary escorted the twins into Mr. Parker's big office.

"Hello ladies! Teyona and Keyona right?"

"Yes sir."

"Which one is which?"

"I'm Teyona and this is my sister Keyona!"

"Well ladies… it's a pleasure to meet you both. I do wish that we could have met under different circumstances, and please except my deepest condolences. Your father was a very good friend of mine, as well as a very good man, please have a seat ladies.

Now I know that this situation is very hard for you to deal with, and it never pleases me to bare witness to other people's problems and pain, but as an attorney, it's my job to try to comfort them and help them make the best choices to better their lives and future.

Your father's main concern in life was your well being, and he trusted me with a lot of money and I helped him establish a stable bank account for you both overseas. Attorney Parker handed both girls and envelope with their names on it, and when the twins saw what name was on the envelope that he gave them, they traded envelopes and the attorney said, "excuse me", the twins opened up the envelopes and they had a oversea's account in the amount of one million dollars. Now your money is drawing interest at seven percent and it hasn't been up graded in about eight months since we first established it, so you can practically imagine what you got now?"

"Thank you Sir," Keyona said.

"Now, I'm your attorney for life, so if you ever need my assistance for anything, then just ask. I'm here for you!"

"Well do you deal with real estate?" Teyona asked.

"Yes I do, as a matter of fact; I sold your father both of his houses. I believe that they are both in your names."

"Yes, we found the deeds! And we will like to sell them both, because we're about to relocated to a different state and start over."

"I understand. I can have them both appraised and on the market within two weeks, if that's good enough for you?"

"That would be excellent, Keyona said. We will have everything moved out in a week and send you a copy of the keys and paperwork."

"That sounds great Ms. Fox."

"Also, here's an invitation to our fathers funeral if you can make it, if not, then we clearly do understand."

"Thank you Ms. Fox, and I will surely try my best."

"The twins stood up and shook his hand and said, it was a pleasure sir, and we will keep in touch."

"Please do and the pleasure was truly mine." Said attorney Parker as the twins smiled and walked out of his office.

* * * *

As they got back in the 600 Benz Coup, Keyona said, "Damn Tey, Tey, daddy was ballin!"

"I know, and he made sure that he looked out for us too. Damn I miss him so much!"

"Well, let's go get something to eat before we have to go and pick up grandma at 11:00 a.m."

"That sounds good…I need something in my system before I fall out. All we been eating is junk food."

"I know, we're going to be looking like some fat rich-ladies in the Bahamas with a bikini bathing suit on!"

"You're crazy! I'm not going out like that, as soon as this is over with, I'm going to get me a lifetime membership at a fitness center and keep it tight..!"

And they both started laughing as they drove off out of the parking lot.

* * * *

Grandma Fay's airplane arrived on schedule, and as she walked through the airport terminal, she instantly spotted her two beautiful grand-daughters as they ran up to her and kissed her with tears in their eyes and embraced her.

"Look at my babies," grandma Fay said as she held both girls in a tight embrace.

"Hi grandma," the twins said as they took in all of the tender love that their grandmother had for them.

"Wow babies, look at both of you, you girls has gotten so big and beautiful, you're not grandma's little baby girls no more, you're my little ladies now."

The twins smiled as they notice the redness that filled their grandma eyes.

"Let's go grab your luggage and get out of here."

"O'kay babies." Fay said as they walked over and grab her luggage and left the airport.

Once in the car Fay said, "wow this is a nice car ain't this one of those 600 Benz Coups?"

"Yes, it was daddy's hooptie, he called it his hoe catcher." And they all started laughing!

"What did Lala call it," Fay asked?

"You know Lala, she didn't trip-she just always drove it to let all of the Hoochies who was jockin daddy know that she was his number one."

"That's my Lala," Fay said. "Now tell me what exactly happened, and I want the raw and uncut version!"

Keyona was driving and Teyona was in the passenger seat. Keyona looked at Teyona and Teyona said, "I'll tell her."

Teyona turned around in her seat so that she could look at Fay in her eyes and than said, "Well grandma, we all was sitting at the kitchen table trying to get daddy to buy me and Keyona some sounds and rims to go with the brand new Cadillac Escalade truck that daddy said that he was going to buy for us, as a graduation gift. It was our

58

Prom Day, and we were just kicking it enjoying the good vibes, when we heard a knock at the door.

Lala got up to answer it, and four masked men with guns ran in on us. Daddy jumped up and tried to go for his gun that he keep in his back, but this big man shot daddy twice in the stomach as soon as he ran in. Daddy fell to the floor, and me and Keyona jumped on top of daddy to try to shield him from anymore bullets, than I tried to grab daddy's gun but, the big robber stomp me hard in the back with his boot and knocked me off daddy. Then he snatched the gun out from daddy's back-belt. The other robbers started dragging everybody around the room and putting plastic restraints on us. Then the big man started asking daddy for the rest of the dope and money, but because daddy had just stacked up a bird at the table in ounces, daddy told him that, that was all that he had. But, big man didn't believe daddy, and told the other robbers to search the house.

The big man then went over to Lala and started raping her." Teyona pulsed as her eyes glared down into the back seat of the car as her mind visualized the whole incident. Then she said, "Lala, must have slipped her hands out of her restraints because, she started tussling with the big man for his gun and while they were wrestling over the gun, the other robber ran up and shot Lala in the face and blow half of it off. When Lala hit the ground, the robber shot Lala again in the chest.

The big man who cause Lala's death just started laughing as the other robber argued about how, 'he didn't come here for that rape shit.' But, the big man wasn't trying to hear that because he said, 'I DID,' and went over to Keyona and started trying to rape her.

The other robbers who were standing there started laughing as they watched Keyona trying to fight the big man off. But just then, I was able to slip my restraints off, (as Teyona held up her hands to show her grandmother the scratches and bruises from the restraints) then Teyona continued; when I got my hands loose I seen the butt of the gun that daddy kept under the couch, so I grabbed it and shot the first robber in the chest…he was the one who shot Lala. He dropped his gun as the impact from the blast knocked him against the wall. Then, I aimed the gun at the big man who was trying to rape Keyona, and shot him dead off in his head, and blow his brains out.

The robber, who was standing right there watching, ran and jumped out of the big picture window in front. I shot at him, but missed, and he got away. I ran into the bedroom to get the robber who was in there searching for the dope, but he had already jumped out-of the bedroom window, and as I looked out of the window I seen both robbers ran and hop into a green Regal and sped away. I ran back into the living-room where Keyona was kneeling over daddy, he was still alive, and he told us to take the dope and money out of the house before the police arrived, and said for us to go to the safe-house.

Then he gave us the combination to the safe and told us that, that was our money now, and for us to watch each-other's backs and don't trust nobody. Those was his last words, then he died in Keyona's arms. I ran over to Lala and she was also alive, but half her face was gone and she was shot in the chest too! She asked us was daddy dead? I said 'yeah,' she said that she didn't want to live life like that and asked me to kill her!"

Teyona pulsed and looked down and then back into Fay's eyes and said, "I went to get the robber's gun, and shot her in the heart so she wouldn't have to suffer no more!"

Fay cupped Teyona's hand and said, "you did the right thang," then she looked into her grand-daughters eyes as Teyona's fought to hold back the tears from falling from her eyes and she smiled at her with love.

"After that, Teyona begin speaking again, I took the same big gun that the robber used to shoot Lala in the face with-'the police said that it was a 44 bull dog or something like that', but I took it and unloaded it into his face, and then I took the other gun that I found under the couch, which was daddy's 357 magnum, and I shot the big man who raped Lala in the dick and blow it clear off. I was mad that I only had one bullet left in the gun. Anyway, after that, I grabbed the dope and money and gave it to Key, Key, and told her to meet me at the stash spot, and when she left, I called the police, but they pulled up as I was calling. I told them everything but left out the part about the dope and Key, Key being there. I told them that Key, Key was at her auntie's house.

Keyona pulled up in the stash house driveway, and parked as Fay said, "well I'm glad that you two made it out safe, and you did right baby, I just wish that you would have killed every one of them basters."

Keyona looked over at Teyona and as their eyes met Keyona said, "Tey, Tey, that's grandma, you can tell her, you know that if anybody is down with us, then it's her!"

"Tell me what?" Fay said, as Teyona looked at Fay and they made eye contact. "Baby you can tell me anything! I'm going to always be down with you, whether right or wrong! I'm going to support you and be down for you both, you're my babies and all that I got left in this world. So please don't ever question my loyalty to you both, because I'm going to always ride with you."

"I feel you grandma, let's go in the house and I'll tell you the rest in there."

They all got out of the car as Teyona and Keyona grabbed Fay's luggage and they went into the house to relax a little better.

"Do you want something to drink grandma," Keyona asked?

"Yeah, I can use a shot of Hennessy if you got any?"

"Yeah we got some....you know that daddy kept that!"

"Get me a glass too Key, Key." Teyona said as everyone started to laugh.

"Everyone sat down and enjoyed a glass of Hennessy as Teyona put their grandmother up on how they found out about who all was involved in the conspiracy to kill their father, and how they killed Tate and Teddy in the motel room, and how they plan on getting revenge for their father's and Lala's death.

"Fay said, "Now that's my babies!" And leant over and hugged Teyona and Keyona. "That's right, ain't nobody going to get away with killing one of ours!"

Keyona smiled and looked at Teyona and said, "I told you that grandma was just like you."

And Teyona laughed and said, "from now on grandma we're going to call you G-Mom!"

Everyone started laughing as Fay said, "yeah, I like that! Now who do we get next?"

"Wait a minute G-Mom, Keyona said let me and Tey, Tey, handle this!"

"Girl please, I've put down a couple of drive-byes in my days, and sold dope majority of my life. You forgot that I was raised in the ghetto's and I raised my son in the projects, so I've done seen and been through it all. If it wasn't for your daddy hustling and taking care of me, I'd still be slinging and getting money. Don't get it twisted ya'll, who do you think raised your daddy to be the down nigga he was? That was my one and only, and nigga's is going to die behind this shit! As a matter of fact, I got in touch with my brother's youngest son Red Rum out of Shreveport Louisiana, and he's on his way down here. Him and your father was real close, and a couple of years a part, and he didn't take this ordeal that lightly. He's the leader of a gang called Murder Mafia, and they been known to live up to there name," and Fay winked her eye.

"G-Mom, we don't need a whole lot of people in our business, because it might create too much attention and get us all caught up," Teyona said.

"Don't be silly girl, that's exactly what we need to create some sort of diversion and keep the police off your tracks. You feel me?"

"She has a point there Tey, Tey! This way we can handle ours on the down low, while the police think that it's some sort of gang war. Big Al click is from the Tre, Tre's, so we can make it seem as though them and the Crenshaw mafia's is at war while we're doing are thing."

"That might work, but you forgetting about one thing," said Teyona.

"What?" Fay and Keyona said together.

"During the time of war – everybody's going to be on point, and we mess up our element of surprise," Teyona said; as she took a sip of Hennessy.

"Well, we just got to hit them hard first, before the war fully get kicked off," Fay said.

"What a minute ya'll," Keyona said…. G-Mom, I respect that gangsta shit that you got in your heart, but we got to be smart about our every move. See what we ain't told you about yet is the money that daddy left us! We got over $600 thousand dollars in cash, and $150 thousand dollars in his business account that the beauty salon and clothing store made within a year, plus daddy put me and Tey, Tey, a million dollars in an overseas bank account that we just found out about. So we're trying to make it out of here alive, and without becoming fugitives so we can enjoy it. Now let's be smart about it, and set up an escape plan. I say, we need you G-Mom, to go and buy us a house in California, so we can go to in case of an emergency. That way if all shit breaks loose, and the police catch onto us, then we can at least run away and have a chance to enjoy life before we get caught or die!"

"I'm feeling you on that Key, Key! Teyona said.

Also, we need to get some fake identification and social security numbers, and pass ports and I know just the person! They charge 5g's for the whole hook up, and that way, G-Mom can hook up our new business and residence in our alias, and that way if we got to run, then we can stay under the radar."

"That's a smart idea, but I got to get one of those nigga's for what they did to my son, or I'm not going to be able to live life comfortable no more! After that, I'll leave and get everything situated o'kay?" Fay said as she tried to negotiate her position.

Teyona looked at Keyona and said, "How can we argue with that!"

"I guess that you're right, but we got to plan it to a tee, and G-Mom, you got to start acting a little more timid and naive, or people is going to get suspicious."

"O'kay – but, this Hennessy got my blood boiling. I guess I can play the religious type, how's that?"

"I guess that will have to do, but be cool with it G-Mom," Keyona said as they all laughed. "Now let's go get our hair done and hit the Aurora Mall so we can grab some clothes for the funeral."

* * * *

They went to the beauty salon and had the ladies there hook them up with a fresh fly hair style, along with a manicure and pedicure. Then they stopped at the mall and grabbed some expensive black dresses that looked-alike for the funeral, and had dinner at a fine restaurant together and enjoyed their grandma's company.

They made it back home at 9:30 p.m. and each of them took a warm bath to relax, and then they sat around and talked the night away. The twins filled G-Mom in on everything that they knew about Big Al and gang. Big Al was by far the biggest dope dealer in that part of Denver, and he could snap his fingers and have killers gunning for them if he ever found out that they posed a threat to him, so they had to be very careful and figure out the right way to make their move on him.

They agreed that G-Mom should rent an apartment in the cut for Red Rum when he got there, because Teyona didn't trust him like that to let him stay with them, and the less contact they had with him the better. So after the funeral they would go rent him a cool apartment out of the way.

"Listen ya'll, we got a long day ahead of us tomorrow, so I got to get some rest, here G-Mom," Teyona said as she handed G-Mom a 3.80 automatic and said, "it was Lala's, so make sure that it gets used right!" G-Mom nodded her head yes, and smiled at her.

"Don't worry baby, it's going to get some rec!" And they started busting up at each other, Keyona just shook her head and said, "I don't know what I'm going to do with you two!"

Chapter 6
They Call Me Trouble, and with Me is Problems!

The day of the funeral was a sad day for them all, but the twins took pride in preparing a nice expensive funeral. They rented an all white caravan with a limousine and two hearses. They tied two red bandanas on each one of the vehicles antennas, to let the world know that their father belong to a blood gang. And they drove their caravan down Colorado Blvd onto Martin Luther King Blvd to represent, and to burn the eyes of all the haters.

"Look at that shit there, Little C said, to Jim, Jim and Sparks as they seen the caravan pass. Cuzz, we should light that muthafucka up! I don't know who the fuck them bitches think they're playing with," Little C said; as he through up his sign letting the caravan know that he was from Tre Tre.

"Man, leave them dead muthafucka alone, this crazy nigga's banggin on the dead." Jim, Jim said to Sparks as they started laughing.

Fuck that shit Cuzz... I'll bang on a nigga if he's dead or alive, it don't matter to me. I'm just mad that I didn't kill'em!" Little C said.

As the caravan passed Little C and them, Teyona seen Little C throw up his set and bang on the caravan, and she looked at Keyona and said, "Key, Key remind me to kill that little bitch." Keyona shook her head as they all rode in silence.

The twins didn't invite too many people, just the ones who they knew that their father and Lala liked. Nevertheless, the flower arrangements was beautiful, a hundred dozen of red roses high-lighted the scene. Both of them was layed in red and gold caskets and they put their father in a new $3,000 dollar red Vasachie suit with a black silk shirt and tie. Lala had a closed casket, but she was still dressed in a thousand dollar red silk Vasachie dress.

The preacher gave a deep sermon, and the gospel singers turned it out. The twins and Fay said their final farewell. And then they lowered the caskets into the ground. The twins brought a family volt, to add three more spaces next to their father and Lala's resting place, and hoped that they won't have to occupy it no time soon. The funeral was over and the ladies all walked away with one thang on their minds, revenge!

After the funeral was over, the limo driver dropped them back off at the stash spot. It was still early so they decided to jump into the Benz, and go see about renting a plush one bedroom apartment for Red Rum in an upscale location. But first they wanted to stop by their old house on there way back. As they opened the door, a flash-back of all the hidden pain came flooding out, and took them by surprise. And they broke down and began crying like babies as they looked around the room and seen the blood stain rug and furniture still in the house. And their thoughts burned as they remembered what took place that horrible night.

They rushed to pack the majority of their clothes and valuables that were left in the house because; they know that it would be a long time before they would return back to that house again.

As they left the house and got back into the car Keyona said, "I'll call cousin Fred and have him come by tomorrow and see if he could get a cleaning crew or someone to clean the blood up, and I'll have him put everything else in storage."

Teyona didn't say a word, she just kept looking out of the passenger side window with revenge written all over her face. Keyona looked through the rear view mirror, and saw Fay wiped a tear from her eye as Keyona drove off.

It wasn't a question about what was about to go down, the smell of blood was still in their nose, and death was embedded in their hearts and mind.

* * * *

Everybody was tired as they made it back to the stash spot, so they all layed down and got a little rest, as they nurtured the pain that just tortured their spirit.

Keyona awoke at 10 o'clock that night, and notice that Teyona was gone. She got up and glanced into the guest bedroom were G-Mom was sleeping, and as G-Mom saw Keyona standing in the dark doorway. Keyona said, "Hey G-mom, you woke?"

"Yeah baby, I just woke up around 20 minutes ago."

"Have you seen Tey, Tey?" Keyona asked as G-Mom got up from the bed and walked over to her.

"No baby, I ain't seen her."

Keyona walked over to the window with G-Mom right behind her, and she looked out of the window and seen that the Vett was gone. "She took the Vett," Keyona uttered.

"Key, Key, she'll be alright! One thing that I can say about Tey, Tey, she knows how to handle herself." G-Mom said as she giggled and walked over to the bar and made them a shot of Hennessy, and walked back over to Keyona and said, "here baby, relax, we're going to be alright." Keyona smiled and went over to the stereo and took out her Biggie Smalls CD and place it in the stereo. Then she went to go sit next to her grandmother on the couch.

"G-Mom, you ain't aged a bit!"

"Girl you know that we got good gene's and I'm a ghetto girl, so we stay in shape because we run the street a lot!" And they both laughed.

"G-Mom, do you need some money?"

"No baby I'm fine, your daddy kept a safe at my house too! I think that it's around 80g's in it."

Eighty thousand ain't enough money to live good off of....when you leave we're going to send you back with a few hundred g's and daddy's new 600 Benz. That way if all else fall, then you'll be well off in life."

"Baby, my life wouldn't be worth living without ya'll"

We love you too G-Mom, but please don't base your life on our life outcome. We've devoted our life to getting revenge for our father's and Lala's death. So if we die in the process, then we achieved our goals, because you can bet, we won't die alone."

"Listen Key, Key, ain't none of us going to die, they're gonna be the one's having the next funerals, not us! We're gonna be gone before they know what hit them, so get that thought out of your mind."

The front door opened and Teyona walked in with a Walmart and Sears bag. Damn Tey, Tey, you can tell somebody when you leave out." Keyona said.

"Key, Key, I ain't going to live my life all scared and shit….If I'm going to die, then just bury me with my father and Lala, and go on with your life. I'm not with all that paranoid stuff."

Keyona looked at her sister and knew that she made all the sense in the world and said, "you're right Tey, Tey, but still you should have enough respect and understanding to know that I'm gonna worry about you. Too much is going on and we just came out of a tragic ordeal."

"Not as tragic as it's gonna get!" Teyona said, then she looked at her sister and knew how she was always over protective and said, "I know you're right Key, Key, I should've let you know, but I couldn't sleep, so I went shopping to grab us some stuff. Don't worry, next time I'll leave a note or some shit like that…! Now look what I got for us." She opened up the paper bags and poured all the stuff out. She had three band new pairs of brownie gloves, some black ski masks, a Halloween mask, three big black jackets, some duck tape, plastic restraints, and a small axe.

"Damn girl, are you sure that this is the first time that you did this? G-Mom asked and Teyona just smiled at her.

"Believe me, she's a natural." Keyona said, as she looked at G-Mom with a wide eye facial expression.

"That's my baby!" G-Mom said, as Teyona started blushing, and Keyona just shook her head.

"Listen, I passed by the dope street on Colfex and I seen that nigga Little Sam out there serving. I was temped to bust a u-turn and go back and serve him, but I figured that it would be best to stick to the plan so we can have a better chance at getting them all. It don't make no sense in taking a risk of being seen and risking the surprise."

"Smart move!" Keyona said.

"Also, I stopped by my friend's house who does the fake ID's and she said for us all to stop by the DMV at 8:30 tomorrow morning so she can hook us up. She said, for us to know what names we want already, and she'll have us plugged up within a week with everything. I paid her half already and told her that we'll give her the other half when she finish everything. G-Mom, I paid for you one too, because you might want to leave with us. That's if you think that you'll like living in the Bahamas?"

"Baby I'll roll with ya'll to hell if that's were we got to go, I just want to be with my family – but the Bahamas' do sound nice!" And the twins started laughing. Then G-Mom reached into her bra and pulled out a fat sack of purple crush weed, and said do you girls got some Zig Zags around here?"

"G-Mom, you brung that weed on the plane with you? Keyona said with a surprise look on her face.

"Of course baby, you know that we got a special glove compartment." And her and Teyona started busting-up laughing as Keyona looked at them confused!

"She put it in her coochie girl." Teyona explained, as Keyona put her hand over her mouth and fell-out laughing.

"I'll grab you some G-Mom, I think that I seen some in daddies weed box." And Teyona walked into the bedroom to get the Zig Zags.

"You ain't lying G-Mom… you're as ghetto as all out doors!" Keyona said as they both started laughing.

"G-Mom rolled her a fat joint and the twins took a hit of it to catch a small buzz, "Damn, this shit is the bom G-Mom." Keyona said.

"Don't even go there ya'll." Teyona said as she read their mind and knew that they was laughing because G-Mom had it in her pussy, so they tried to make it seem like that's why it was so good, and strong.

"G-Mom, come on let me show you our guns," Teyona said, as they smiled and took G-Mom into the closet, and opened the hidden door that stored all the guns behind it.

"Wait, here, put these on." Teyona said, as she handed G-Mom a pair of new brownie gloves.

"G-Mom put on her gloves and grabbed two twin 45 automatics, and said, "Now this is what I'm talking about. This is what I need right here!

"It's two extra clips for them right there." Keyona said as she pointed to the two clips.

"Can I have these?" G-Mom asked.

"Sure, if that's what you want! We're going to set this thang off, so you better get what you're comfortable and familiar with." Teyona said as she smiled.

"This will work for me, and she grab the hollo points – yeah, this is me!" G-Mom said as she pointed them and check the clips and made sure that a bullet was in the chamber.

"I see that you know how to operate them." Keyona said.

"Of course, who do you think taught your daddy how to shoot!" G-Mom said as Keyona looked at Teyona and Teyona started laughing.

"I thought that I was your twin! Keyona said, that's your damn twin right there!" And everyone started busting up.

* * * *

The next day they got up in the morning and went to the DMV and filled out the identification slips and took new photos. After that, G-Mom's had the girls stop by the liquor store, and she ran in and brought her a auto buy news paper and a six pack of Millers genuine draft. They sat in the car as G-Mom's looked for a nice car in the news paper.

"G-Mom, if you need a car then we can rent you one." Keyona said.

"No baby, this is for something else. Here we go....Prefect!" And then G-Mom jumped out of the car and went to the pay phone and made a call.

"G-Mom's is kind of burned out Tey, Tey."

"Naw, she just got a lot of game, and been through a lot in her life. Can you imagine all that she experienced in her life? That's a thoroughbred there! And she's down to the fullest!"

"You ain't lying about that." Keyona said as G-Mom came back to the car.

G-Mom got in and handed Teyona a piece of paper with an address on it. And said, "Take me here, and I need $3,500 dollars." Keyona went into her purse and counted out $35 hundred dollars and handed it to G-Mom.

Teyona pulled off and pulsed at the stop sign as she seen a brand new Blue Bentley G.T. pull up sitting on 22 inch chrome rims and beating. Big Al jumped out as the Twins looked at him and he gazed at them and waved. Keyona said, "smile, and beep the horn, and drive off," and Teyona complied as she turned the corner and drove off.

"Who was that G-Mom asked?"

"That was Big Al," Keyona said.

"That's him – why you didn't say anything?" G-Mom said in an aggressive tone.

"Because we got to stick to our plan G-Mom," Keyona firmly said.

"You're right!" G-Mom's said in a soft voice.

They pulled up to the address and G-Mom's said "ya'll wait here, I'll be back in like 20 minutes."

Then she jumped out of the car and went up to the address that was on the paper. She knocked on the door and an old white man walked out and showed G-Mom an old school convertible, 1988 Mustang G.T., then she jumped behind the wheel and he got in on the other side and they drove off. Fifteen minutes later they were back, and G-Mom went inside the old man's house.

"I wonder what she's up too?" Keyona said in an inquisitive tone.

"I don't know, but you better believe that it's a purpose behind it." Teyona said as G-Mom came out of the old man's house and jumped into the Mustang and pulled up along side the 600 Benz, and said, "Let's go get the rent-a-car now, I'll follow you." And Teyona pulled off and lead the way to the rent-a-car place. Keyona ran into the rent-a-car place and rented a new 2007 two door black Trans Am. And they caravanned back to the stash spot.

When they got back to the house Keyona asked G-Mom, "Who you got the Mustang for, your Nephew?"

"No baby, we need a G-ride if we're gonna get at these nigga's."

"But ain't that car going to get traced back to you, if we do something in it?" Keyona asked.

"Baby, I didn't give him my real information. I told him that I lost my ID and that I'm waiting for the DMV to shoot me another one, but I seen the ad for the Mustang in the paper and I always wanted one, so I thought that I should come and buy it before someone else beats me to it. He didn't care, all he wanted was the money, and for me to sign the bill of sale. Now if we get pulled over before we do something, all the police is going to do is tell us to go get it registered. And once we do something in it, then we can just abandon it, and burn it, and it can't be trace back to us!" "I told you that G-Mom was game oriented." Teyona said.

"Yeah, she's vicious too!" Keyona said as they laughed and G-Mom's cell phone ranged.

She answered it and said, "O'kay baby, we'll be right there," and hung up and said, "Red Rum is at the Comfort Inn Motel on Colorado Blvd. Room 187!"

The ladies jumped into the rent-a-car and headed over to where G-Mom's nephew Red Rum was. They pulled up into the Comfort Inn parking lot and parked, and as they got out G-Mom seen the look on Teyona's face and said, "don't worry baby, I wouldn't even call anyone that I

81

didn't trust one hundred percent. He's kind of crazy, but real, and down for the cause, so let him play his part, and we'll play ours!"

Teyona shook her head in a "yes" manner, and they knocked on the door. When the door opened a real dark skin brother with a bald head and gold teeth answered the door. He stood around 5' 11", and was a nice medium built.

He said, "Hey Auntee Fay, how's my favorite Auntee doing?" With a slight southern draw to his tone. "Come in ya'll, come in!"

The girls walked in as he said come and give me a hug ya'll, my condolences little momma - don't' worry, ain't no one going to get away with disrespecting my family like that! We come to bring the muthafucken pain. By the way, this is Itty Bitty my closes friend and devoted comrade, and this is Nina my loyal love interest. They both is apart of this Murder Mafia movements, and totally devoted to me, so you know that they are as thorough as they came. Now have a seat and tell me everything that happened and what you've found out since then.

Keyona gaze at Nina who was a real pretty Cubin lady with long silky black curly hair, and a beautiful bronze complexion to go with her nice sista built. Itty Bitty was a little dude about 5'7" with a slim built, and Teyona thought to herself, "this dude looks harmless. What kind of crew is this?"

Teyona was telling Red Rum about how the attempted robber/murder occurred, but she left out the part about the Tate and Teddy incident, she just said that one of her father's friends put them up on who got away, and why it happened.

Red Rum eyes turned blood shot red, and he said, "listen, we need some guns, and to know where they kick it at, and we'll do the rest."

Teyona smiled and said, "we was thinking that it would be best to make it seem like the Crenshaw Mafia's is beefing with Big Al's click the Tre, Tre, and that way it would create a diversion, because we're going to be handling our business from the other end."

"I feel you little Momma! We don't like crips any damn way, and since the Crenshaw Mafia's didn't bust a cap when this shit occurred, then it's only right that we make them participate." And him and his crew started laughing as the girls just smiled and shook their heads.

"Well, listen Red Rum, we went and got ya'll a nice apartment out a little ways, so you can be secured and low key while you're putting in your work."

"Is that right – now that's the love that I'm speaking of, now we can do it right!" And him and Itty Bitty looked at each other and laughed.

Red Rum jumped in the rent-a-car with Teyona and G-Mom, and Keyona jumped in the Trans Am with Itty Bitty and Nina. Nina drove and followed Teyona and Teyona took the scenic route, and showed Red Rum and his crew all the dope strips and main streets.

"Look, see him, that's Paper..... that's the nigga that my daddy shot at the club and Big Al's lieutenant. I think that he could have been the one pushing the issue on my father." Teyona said to Red Rum as they passed by the liquor store and seen Paper getting out of this nice dark blue Range Rover Truck sitting on 24 inch chrome rims.

They made it to the apartment and when they got in the apartment it was completely empty. Red Rum and his crew looked around as Keyona said, "as you see, we didn't have a chance to put no furniture in it yet, it was kind of a spare of the moment type deal."

"Don't worry about it young tender we probably won't be here that long anyway. Who's name is it in?" Red Rum asked.

"I put it in my name! G-Mom said, "so please don't do nothing in it that can trace back to me, I just wanted you to have somewhere safe to lay your head at, because them motels is like a dead give away."

"Don't worry Fay, I'll use it strictly for resting only!"

"Listen, G-Mom, me and Keyona is gonna go grab them some supplies and something to eat. We'll be back in 30 minutes." Teyona said.

"O'kay babies."

Teyona and Keyona walked out of the door, and Red Rum turned to Fay and said, "Auntee, do you think that they can handle the pressure?"

"They asked me the same thing about you!" Red Rum eyes got big. Then G-Mom said, "listen nephew, them girls is as thorough as they come, and as you see, they got blood on their hands too. Even if you didn't come, Big Al and his crew would've felt their raft, and believe me, them two is the last one's that you would want as your enemies. Ain't nothing like a woman's scorn.... Ain't that right Nina?"

"You got that right Ms. Fay!"

"Call me G-Mom, that's my new nick name!" Red Rum eyes got big as everyone laughed. Fay said, "the girls gave it to me!"

"Well it's official then, 'G-Mom it is'!" Itty Bitty said as everyone agreed shaking their heads yes, and laughing.

Teyona and Keyona stooped and got a bucket of Kentucky Fried Chicken and two pizza's. When they left there they stopped by the liquor store and grabbed two bottles of Hennessy, some Cranberry juice and orange juice, a case of Millers, some gum, chips, and a box of Swiser Sweets. After that, they stopped by the safe house and grabbed a Tec 9, a 44 Desert Eagle, a 357 Magnum, and a Gloc 9mm, all with extra bullets and clips. Teyona also grabbed some stacks of money and a fat bag of their fathers old weed stash, and then, they jumped back into the car and headed back to the apartment.

When they got back to the apartment they knocked on the door. Itty Bitty looked out the peep-hole and seen the twins hands was full of food, and Teyona had a duffle bag thrown over her shoulder.

Keyona said, "go look out in the car and grab the other stuff for us."

Itty Bitty gave her his little handsome boyish smile as he left out. It was obvious that Itty Bitty had a crash on the twins, but since he couldn't tell them apart, he desired them both the same.

Teyona set the food down and opened up the duffle bag, and pulled out three stacks of money wrapped up with rubber bands, and said, "here you go Red Rum, this for you."

"Baby I don't want you money, I'm not here for that! Your father was my only cousin, and we always keep it real with each other. I'm here to avenge his death! I don't care about his money. I'm going to jack a lot of these niggas anyway, so I'm going to get mines regardless – you feel me little Momma?"

Itty Bitty walked back in with the case of beer and paper bags full of liquor and stuff.

"I feel you on that, Teyona said, but this is just to help you get the other things that you may need, so you can do what you have to do. You're going to need a G-ride, and some blankets and shit, so use it for the things that ya'll need, that's all."

"Good looking out little Momma, now let me see what you brung me." Red Rum said as he started pulling out all the guns. He pulled out the Tec 9 first and said, "I see that you know my style." And everyone started to laugh. Then he pulled out the Desert Eagle 44 and Itty Bitty said, "Now that's what I'm talking about," and grabbed the big gun. Then he pulled out the 357 Magnum and grabbed the Gloc 9 mm and gave it to Nina and said, "I know that you feel naked without it."   The twins looked at her with surprise in their eyes.

"Oh, in case you're wondering, Nina here served two years in the Army and was a combat specialist. She received a dishonorable discharge because she stabbed the captain in the dick with an ink pen, when he was trying to rape her. So she's really not feeling what happen to Lala, and she's taking it personal!"

The twins looked an Nina with a lot more respect and appreciation as they all gave a little respectful smile to each other.

"Well ladies, I see that you're on point and that makes the game that much more easier to play. We're going to go grab some stuff from the Walmart down the street, and then it's on! Just watch the News you'll see us. What did you say that drug enforcement officer name was?"

"Detective Jones!" Teyona said, "Watch out for him."

'Okay, let's eat, and then go grab some stuff from Walmart, then we can go check out the territory. Here's my cell phone number if you need me.

"O'kay!"

"O'kay," the girls said as they left.

The girls went home and went over their plans, "now listen Key, Key,.... I need you to be on point! You know that them nigga's is going to run up to the car, tomorrows the first, so it's going to be poppin. As soon as we get out, drop the top, that way it would be easier for us to get in, and then you hit the escape route. G-Mom this is your big day view, so make it count, cause after this, we need you on the highway back to California. You'll take the 600 Benz back with you, and we're putting 400 g's in a suit case in the truck so you can take with you, and that should cover the down payment for the house. We've talked to daddy's attorney, and Mr. Parker said that his friend got us a baby mansion in Hollywood Hills waiting, and he would put it under our alias names. Also, he needs 10 g's for the fictitious corporation for us, and another 60 g's to put in the corporate account under the fictitious corporation. But only 50 g's will be placed in the account, the other 10 g's is what they charge to launder the money for us, any questions?"

"Nope baby, let's just kick this shit off in the right way. Ya'll be careful and keep me posted. You know that I'm gonna be worried and waiting!"

"I know but we're gonna be alright!"

"What do you think about Red Rum and his crew?" G-Mom asked.

"Well he seems cool and sincere, but he don't look like he's got much of a crew." Teyona said as her and Keyona laughed.

"Well don't underestimate him….don't forget that he's the leader of Murder Mafia, and they practically run Shreveport Louisiana. You don't earn that kind of respect from your good looks, 'if you know what I mean.' Just keep an eye on the news so you know, and be able to see his moves. If you need him, then don't hesitate to call him, sometimes it's best to have more people when you're warring with a kingpin! You feel me?"

"Yes G-Mom, I feel you, and if it comes to that, then I will." Teyona said to put and end to the conversation.

The food is ready Keyona said as she brung G-Moms and Teyona a delicious fat stake dinner.

"Thank you baby, this looks good! I didn't know that you knew how to burn like this, G-Mom said with a pleasant smile.

"Yeah, Lala taught us how to get down." Keyona said as she caught her thoughts and the room got quiet as everyone just sat there and ate in silence.

Chapter 7
Let the Games Begin

It was the first of the month, and Big Al was at his stash spot on Federal with his two lieutenant's Paper and Big Cojo, and they was all laughs and smiles as they talked about how their profit nearly double since Kev Dog died.

"Man if I would've known that my profit would have double without that nigga around, then I would've been put his punk ass to rest." Big Al said as they all laughed.

"I wanted to kill him a long time ago, for that bitch shit that he did to me at the club. He's gonna get mad because I grabbed his bitch ass, and he buss on a nigga like a sucka. Shit I was drunk, and that ass was everywhere. I couldn't help it, it was instinct!" He said as they all laughed.

"Well it's a new day now." Big Al said. "We got all of our dope spots clocking damn near double, and the crew got the block poppin' today. That's not including all the niggas who came to us to buy quarters, halves, and whole keys. Shit we might have to take over them Crenshaw Mafia's niggas spots too. If we hit that nigga Damu, Sin, and C.K. up, then we'll damn near run the whole Westside and half of the Southside."

"Shit that might be a good idea, but if we do it, then it should be on the down low, because a war would fuck up our money. We need to make it seem like the Rollin 30's did it, so they will catch the heat and we can kill two birds with one stone." Cojo said.

"That might work too, and if so, we can take over this whole damn town." Paper added.

"Yeah, let me think on it, and I'll get back at you guys on it later on! It looks like I might have to start coping 50 keys a month now, this shit is moving like the wind around here. How many keys do we got left?" Big All asked.

"Only six!" Paper said.

"Well, cook them up and only sale ounces – I'm gonna call Juan and order 30 more. Cojo called Tina and asked her if she's trying to drive down to Texas with me today, and if so, then have her go rent a car and she can follow me."

"O'kay Big Al, I'm on it!"

"How much money is that?" Big Al asked Paper as he finished counting up the stacks of money in front of him.

"That's $160,000 over there, and this is $135,000 over here." Paper said with a big grin.

"O'kay, this is $125,000 right here in front of me, so that's a total of $420,000 thousand dollars!" Now take $30,000 thousand from that stack over there and that would give me $390,000 thousand which would cover the 30 keys that I'm gonna get. Sale the other ounces for $1,050 dollars a pop, that should give us $225,000 thousand dollars give or take – off of them other six birds, and I'll hit ya'll up when I get back with a little extra something to keep your pockets smiling."

"That's right....you know that we got mad love for you right?" Paper asked.

"You better nigga, all this damn money that we're making together. What do you make, $30 thousand a week fucking with me!"

"Something like that!" Paper said with a smile.

"Well take the other 30g's and call up Gwen and get that to her for me. I'll be back tomorrow. I'ma try to do a turn-around this trip." Big Al said.

Cojo walked back into the bedroom and said, "she's down, and she said that she's going to get the rent-a-car now, so she'll be waiting for you."

"Good, I'm out! Big Al grabbed the big suit case and walked out as Cojo and Paper escorted him out to his car.

He put the suit case in the trunk of his new BMW-M5 and rolled out.

Paper and Cojo went back into the stash house, and started cooking up the dope. They loved cooking the dope up when Big Al wasn't around, because they would dry cook it, and put and extra 4 to 5 ounces of baking soda on each key, to stretch it to 40 or 41 ounces a bird. This way, off the six keys, they would make an extra 30 ounces for themselves to spit, and that way they would have some extra money to trick with.

* * * *

The twins pulled up on the dope street on Colfax where Little Sam and some of Big Al's other little workers kick it and serve their rocks at.

Keyona was driving and Teyona was in the passenger seat while G-Mom was laying down in the back seat. They all was dressed in black khaki suits, tennis shoes, base ball hats that covered up their hair, and red bandana's tied to their arms. Teyona and G-Mom both had on ski masks under their base ball hats. And Keyona had on a trick a treat mask, that resemble an old white man.

They rolled up the windows in the Mustang that was tinted and Teyona had her window a couple of inches cracked and she was bent down on the floor in the front seat.

"Hey you got a 50?" Keyona said in a man's voice when she pulled up next to where Little Sam was standing.

Little Sam said, "watch out nigga, I got this one," and he ran up to the car as he saw the profile of a white man through the tinted window.

Keyona lowered the window from the driver side, as Little Sam ran up and Little Sam saw someone jump up with a 12 gauge pointed at him, and he put his hands out to try and stop the gun shot, and the 12 gauge blow his hands clean off his wrist, and he fell to the ground from the impact. Then door to the mustang swung opened and everyone that was standing around was in a daze as to what was going on, just then Teyona jumped out and shot two rounds at the crowd of niggas who was standing around serving. G-Mom was right in back of Teyona as she jumped out with both 45 Automatics in her hands, bussing like an old vet. G-Mom hit the first nigga in the chest as the hollo point dropped him dead on the spot, the nigga next to him was a fat boy, and G-Mom shot him three times in the back and slid him on the concrete as he laid face down in a puddle of blood. G-Mom started shooting everything moving as Teyona lifted the 12 gauge up and pulled the trigger, blowing off Little Sam's face as he was trying to beg for his life. Teyona spotted Little C as he tried to run and jump over a small fence and she shot three times and caught him in mid air, and twisted his body in the air as he hit the grass. Teyona ran up as he was trying to grab his 9mm out of his pocket and when he looked up, he seen Teyona aiming right at him from 6 feet away, and she smiled as she shot two more times, leaving Little C bloody from head to toe. Keyona dropped the convertible top down on the Mustang, and seen the back of a black van door open up and two white men jumped out with guns in hands. G-Mom back was turned as she was shooting at the crowd of nigga's who was hiding behind cars down the street, and shooting back, so Keyona jumped out and hid behind the driver door, as she caught the two police off guard, and started emptying the Mac 10 out on them. She hit them both with a rain of bullets, as G-Mom turned and seen the two white men fall down in back of her, she ran and jumped into the back seat of the Mustang, and popped in her other clips, as Keyona jumped back in the driver seat and waited for Teyona to close her door before she punched out. G-Mom was shooting out of the back seat, and Teyona grabbed the Mac

10 and throw in another clip and shot at the white man
that was laid out on the ground as they sped off.   Keyona
hit three blocks and pulled into an alley, where the rent a
car was parked at, and they jumped out of the Mustang
and grabbed all of the guns and clips and put them in a big
duffle bag. G-Mom and Keyona ran to the rent a car as
Teyona poured a gallon of gas all over the Mustang and
set it on fire, and then she ran and jumped in the rent a car
that was parked at the other end of the alley in the cut, and
jumped in as Keyona drove off and jumped on the
freeway.

They seen the police helicopter off toward the incident
and Keyona pulled off the freeway as Teyona jumped out
and went to throw the mask that they place in a plastic bag
into a big trash dumpster. Then they went to another
location four blocks down and throw the clothes that they
were wearing into another trash dumpster in a trash bag.
They drove home and took a shower to wash the gun
powder residue off them. Teyona took out the Windex
and cleaned all of the guns real good and went to bury
them in different places. When she got back, G-Mom and
Keyona was dressed and smoking a joint. They past it to
Teyona and she hit it and they all just busted out laughing.

G-Mom said, "you girls is 'double trouble'… Keyona you saved our ass back there, that was the damn police. Where in the hell did they come from?"

"They jumped out of the back of that van…! And when I seen them it tripped me out. I knew that ya'll didn't see them, so I had to do something! So I said, 'fuck it', and started bussin' at them."

"Where in the hell did you learn how to shot like that?"

"My daddy taught us!"

Teyona, you're wild girl..! You gave them ever bit of what they deserved. You blew that basters head right off! Which one was that? G-Mom asked.

"That was that nigga Little Sam, and I got that other nigga Little C too!"

"Who is Little C?" G-Mom asked.

"That's the nigga who throw up the gang signs when we passed by in the funeral caravan."

"O'kay, I remember his little ass now! That's what his little disrespectful ass gets." G-Mom said as everyone laughed.

"G-Mom, it's time for you to hit the highway! It was fun having you with us, but we need you to go get everything ready for us, so we can disappear when this is over." G-Mom held her head down looking sad.

"Don't worry G-Mom we got this, and we'll be alright! Tey, Tey's right, we got to have you handle that on the other end for us, or we might get caught up, if we gotta run and ain't got no where to run."

"O'kay babies, but keep me informed and I want ya'll to call me everyday to let me know that ya'll cool. O'kay?"

"Alright G-Mom, we will." Keyona said, as they all hugged.

"Listen G-Mom, you got four hundred thousand dollars in the trunk of your car, so don't be speeding, o'kay?"

"I won't."

"And here!" Teyona gave her a envelope.

G-Mom opened it and it was the pink slip to the 600 Benz Coup and a bill of sale signed over to her.

"I don't know what to say!"

"Honey, there's nothing to say! You're our heart, and we want you to have something nice that daddy left behind."

"I got something nice already that your daddy left me behind." And they all smiled.

"Well let me go pack my clothes so I can get out of here. And I want you to know, that you girls have given me a special memory that I will always treasure, and I love you both so much!"

"We love you to G-Mom," and they all embraced in a family hug.

* * * *

The news caster said, "it's been a horrible day in the streets of Denver as a rival gang jumped out on Colfax street..."

"Itty Bitty cut that up man!" Red Rum said as they were in the apartment planning their moves, they was watching the news on a little 13 inch TV when Itty Bitty reached over and cut up the volume so they could hear better.

"And started shooting everyone in sight. This was known as a drug street where young black men hustle by selling rock cocaine and weed. Little did anyone know that the detectives from the Denver Drug Task Force, had the street under surveillance at the time of the shooting, and when the officers jumped out to try to detain the incident, the rival gang turned their guns on them, and the officers died at the scene, along with seven other young black males who was known gang members and drug dealers. There are no suspects as of yet, and the Denver police is asking anyone who may have any information to call 1-800- S-N-I-T-C-H..!

Excuse me Detective Jones, can you tell us any information on this tragic incident?"

"We have not finish our investigation as of yet, but when we do, then we will deliver a full news report. Now please excuse me."

"That was Detective Jones from the Drug Enforcement Task Force, and as you see, they haven't a clue as of yet."

"Man, that's that damn detective that Teyona said to watch out for." Red Rum said.

"Damn, them girls put in some major work, we might ought to recruit them..!" Itty Bitty said as they laughed.

"Yeah, you ain't lying, can you imaging them with my Nina here together. Boy that would be like opening up hell's gates." And they laughed as Red Rum lend over and kissed Nina.

"I like them, they got heart, and looks to go with it." Itty Bitty said with a smile as he fantasized about how good it would be to have them both.

"Listen, they kicked it off now, so we got to make sure that we make it official. It's time for a diversion. Let's roll."

They pulled up at the liquor store in Tre Tre hood, and saw three young gang members standing in the parking lot sagging with blue khakis on, and Itty Bitty said, "I got this, just keep the car running."

It was 12:30a.m. Eleven hours after the girls shoot out. The police was already gone from the crime scene and the blood on the ground was barely dry. Itty Bitty walked up to the three gang bangers, and caught them off guard as he said, "this is Mafia territory now nigga," and started bustin' at them with his little 3.80 automatic that he brung with him when he came. He hit one in the chest as he fell holding his chest, then he hit one twice in the legs, and the other one in the head, and watch him fall as he ran off and jumped back in the G-ride that they just stole, Red Rum laughed and drove off. They pulled two blocks away and ran and jumped in the car with Nina, as Nina drove back to the apartment where they kicked back and enjoyed a good laugh. Itty Bitty and Red Rum layed back sipping on some Hennessy watching Itty Bitty's big hit movie solo on TV.

The next day Keyona woke up at 7:00 o'clock and turned on the news. She watched the report on their little escapade, and saw that the police considered it a gang related shot out. She smiled as she yarned and looked over at her sister who was still asleep. Then she saw the scene on TV flash to the other shooting, and they also considered it a gang related incident. They said that one man died at the scene from a gun shot wound to the head the second man was in critical condition and the third man just suffered minor gun shot wounds to the legs. Keyona looked over and seen Teyona looking up at the TV listening to the report.

"Do you think that that was Red Rum and them?"

"I doubt it. I think that they will bring it much harder then that. That was probably just some real gang beef shit."

"You're probably right." Teyona said as she yarned and stretched.

"How do you feel this morning Tey Tey?"

"Great..! I feel like a weight has been lifted up off of my heart. But it's still heavy, so I know that I won't be totally content until we get the main niggas involved."

"What's the plan?" Keyona asked.

"We might have to play this one by ear, because we got to get a trace on Big Al and Paper before we can move."

"What about that nigga Cojo?"

"He's apart of their crew ain't he?" Teyona said.

"Yeah."

"Well then, we lay his bitch ass down too." And Teyona smiled as she grabbed her sister hand and said, "you know that I'm proud of you right? You've always been there when I needed you." Keyona smiled as Teyona gave her a big sisterly hug.

"You're my soulmate, so you know that I'ma ride with you, and for you! Against all odds Tey, Tey!"

"Yap, it's us against all odds Key, Key." They smiled as they laid in the bed and talked and planned for the next hour.

* * * *

Big Al was still laying in the bed at 8:30 that morning tripping about the news that Cojo and Paper called and told him about, regarding the drive by shooting. Tina was hard at work butt naked giving him some head, trying to ease his stress. Tina was a stripper and built like a girl who use to be chubby as a kid, but matured into a nice thick sexy lady with very seductive curves. She was a dark brown skin, and was known for her bom head game. She was a vicious nypho and Big Al, had her on lock. She kicked it with other members of the crew, but Big Al was the one who called the shots, and she did what ever it took to keep him happy.

Big Al's cell phone rung as it took him out of his trans and he reach over and answered it.

"Hello!"

"Yeah what's up?"

"What?"

"Your bull shitting, who did it?"

"Is that right, JJ said that?"

"Shot in the legs!"

"Listen, I'll be back there later on today. Tell the crew to stay on point, and send some young homies over there to answer there call. I don't know who the fuck they think that they're fuckin' with."

"I'll holla at you when I get back."

Big Al got out of bed with a limp dick. Tina knew that what ever it was, it had to be pretty bad, because his dick went limp in her mouth, and that kind of shit was unheard of..!

* * * *

It was 11:00 o'clock in the morning and CK and Domu was out on their dope street off of Holly, with their young crew of hustlers trying to get the last of the money from the county check recipients. CK saw a young thick white girl who just moved into the neighborhood, walking across the street with her little 5 year old son, looking like they was coming from the store that was around the corner.

"Damn, there she goes, that's that little thick fine young white girl that just moved down the street." CK said to Domu little brother Baby Domu, as they watched her walking by.

"Let me go holla at this young bitch and see what type of time she's on." CK said as he jogged across the street and said, "What's up snow bunny! Can a brother have a moment of your time and mind?"

The white girl stopped as CK approached. "How are you doing beautiful, my name is CK, you just moved around here huh?"

"Yep!"

"Damn baby, what have you been eating that got you all swoll in the back like that?"

The girl laughed and said, "Oh, no you didn't say that! You're crazy!"

"I ain't joken, we need to write that diet down, and put it in a book. The world need to know about that, we'll make millions!" CK said as they both started laughing together.

"You're crazy boy."

"What's your name snow bunny?"

"It ain't no snow bunny!" She said with a fake attitude.

"O'kay then, what is it, you know that a brother's trying to holla...why are you punishing my thoughts like this?"

She laughed and said, "My name is Suzzy, and this is my little man James here."

"Hey little man, can I get some dap?" And little James looked at his hand, and took his Ninja Turtle and throw it through the air, and made a karate sound. Then he ran over to pick it up.

"I see that he's over protective."

"Yeah, that's my little man." Suzzy said as she saw James off to the side of them playing with his little Ninja Turtle.

"Don't go to far baby." Suzzy hollered.

"He's mixed with black ain't he?" CK said with a smile.

She looked at him with a, 'you ain't slick look,' on her face.

"Naw baby, I'm just saying, you got that eye candy going on, and I'm trying to just enjoy your company! You know, take you out sometimes and get to know you better!"

"Well you seem like a nice guy, we might can get together someday and go out, give me your number and I'll call you." Suzzy said as an old school 86 Cadillac Fleetwood pulled up on Baby Domu and the crew, and started bustin' out of the car window. CK grabbed Suzzy and pushed her down on the side of a parked car as he pulled out his 45 automatic.

Suzzy hollered, "JAMES...!"

CK looked over at the little boy standing in the open staring in a daze. CK ran over and grabbed the little boy and started bussin at the Cadillac as he ran over to Suzzy, and throw little James in her arms. Then he jumped back up and started bussin' at the back window of the Caddy as Domu was across the street behind a brick wall, bussin' over the top of the wall at the Caddy with his 9mm. The nigga in the back seat of the Caddy had a Tec 9 and was bussin' wildly, while the nigga in the passenger side was bussin' a 357 desert eagle out of his window. The driver pulled off just as CK was jumping back up from handing little James to Suzzy, and he lit the back of the Caddy up as the back window cracked from the gun shots. Domu emptied his clip into the passenger side of the Caddy as it pulled off.

CK looked over at Suzzy and said, "are you guys a'ight?"

She looked down at little James who was crying and seen that he wasn't shot and said "we're alright! Thank you for saving us." Then she kissed little James and got up, dusting off her clothes.

CK heard Domu call him and he ran across the street. Baby Domu was shot in the shoulder, T-Bone was shot in the stomach and leg, and the old smoker who was copping from him layed on the ground next to T-Bone twisted on the concrete with his chest leaking from four different holes.

"Damn, CK said, as he kneeled down over T-Bone. He got up and ran over to his Black Chrysler 300 sitting on 22 inch chrome rims, and jumped in and pulled over to the side of the street next to where T-Bone and Domu layed and opened up the back door, then jumped out and ran back over to T-Bone and said, "help me with him Domu." Domu ran over to them and they carried T-Bone and put him in the back seat, and CK told Domu to get in and apply pressure to the stomach wound, and then he went over and helped Baby Domu up and put him in the passenger seat, and ran around to the driver side and jumped in as he looked over at Suzzy and said, "go home and you didn't see nothing." She shook her head "yes," and he sped off to take his little homies to the hospital.

CK made it in time to save both of his little homies life. The nurses rushed the youngster into the emergency room, and CK and Domu went and jumped back into their car. They saw all of the blood that was all over them, and inside the car.

"Did you see who it was?" CK asked.

"Yeah, it was that nigga Jim Jim in the back seat, and that nigga Sparks was driving, and I think that that was little Willy who was shooting out of the passenger side window." Domu said.

"Well it's time to turn on the red light special...!" CK said as Domu gave him dap and they drove away.

Domu picked up his cell phone and called G-nut and told him what went down and to give the homies the red light on Big Al and his crew.

Chapter 8
Gang Bangin' For Life

That night Big Al was standing in the center of twenty of his downest comrades and soldiers. Paper and Cojo both had AK's as they stood at the front door and window of Big Al's sister house on Elm St.

"Now listen nigga's, we don't except that type of disrespect from no one. We're the muthafucken Tre Tre's and we run this muthafucken city. How in the fuck is some bloods going to have the audacity to bring there ass to our side of town, and murder our damn homies. It's time to set this muthafucka off cuzz, and I don't mean no damn drive byes. I mean running up and blowing them nigga's head off. This is for our dead homies cuzz! And if a person ain't putting in no work, then don't mention our business to them, we don't need a nigga telling the police our business. YOU HEAR?"

"We hear you cuzz!"

"Now listen, I want three niggas posted up on our dope stripe at all times with AK's, watching the homie's back. And everybody alternate every six hours, so everyone can get some money. Now instead of a thousand and fifty dollars a ounce, I'm gonna give it to ya'll for eight hundred and fifty dollars a ounce. That way ya'll can be able to sell less and make more. Fuck it, I'll take the loss! But if your not putting in work for the cause, then I'ma cut you all the way off. Cojo would regulate your time slots, so stay on point and watch your backs."

"Tre Tre!" Everyone said in unison.

"Cojo listen cuzz," Big Al said as he pulled him to the side. "I want you to grab two down homies and go over to the Rollin 30 Neighborhood and buss on them. But dress in the Crenshaw Mafia colors, and make them think that it's the Mafia's putting it down on them. That way, we will have them getting at these fools too, and we can smash these fools quicker."

"I know exactly what you mean, and considered it done." Cojo said with a scandalous smile.

* * * *

On the other side of town, CK, Domu, and Sin all had their Crenshaw Mafia family in Domu's sister garage.

"Listen Blood, these bitch ass nigga drew first blood, so it's time to paint the muthafucken streets red. I want them nigga's to be extinct around here – you dig? It's about body bags and toe tags for the next whole month. I want these nigga's to know what this Mafia life is really about. It's on sight from now on, so watch your back and keep your eyes peeled while you're on the block serving, and I want nigga's in the cut posted waiting for the ambush. When you go on a mission keep your face off the news, and try not to kill no innocent by standers. That shit bring in to much heat...let them draw the heat, it works better for us."

"Any question?" CK asked.

"Good let's cut on the red light!"

Domu was handing out guns to everybody who needed them.

* * * *

Everyone was walking on egg shells as the war started kickin off. Both sides was loosing soldiers in the war, and the police had orders to stay out of the way and just let them kill each other off. They figured that the gang war was just what they needed to solve there war on crime and gang violence. As long as they were killing each other, then it got rid of the cities problems and troubles. The detectives was just laying back and building cases off certain gang members who they got word on from their snitches. And this way, when the time was right, then they would step in and put the ones who's still around in prison for life. Nevertheless, none of that mattered now,

113

because death was in the air, and murder and survival was the only thing that the young gang members focus on.

* * * *

Paper was going around making all the drop off's and pick up's from all of the spots and crew members. Red Rum and his crew spotted him as he passed them up on his way to the liquor store. Red Rum said, "Bingo," as they jumped behind the Range Rover in their new G-ride. Red Rum stayed at a cool distant as he saw Paper pull into the liquor store. He looked over at Nina and said, "baby this is your show, here's the extra key to the room if he bites, then we'll meet you at the motel o'kay."

"O'kay Poppy." Nina said as she gave Red Rum a kiss and got out of the car and walked into the store switching with her sexy J-low jeans, high hills, and nice thin silk shirt that vaguely showed off the firmness of her pretty titties, as they stood erect seductively through the thin material.

Itty Bitty watched Nina walk away from the car and said, "that nigga is as good as dead, who can pass up that beautiful monster there! I'm glad that she's on our side!" And Red Rum started rolling, as he parked down the street, so he could see them come out of the store.

"Damn, hey beautiful, hold up, can I look at you for a minute?"

Nina gave Paper her little innocent blush and said, "excuse me."

"No excuse me! Honey my name is Paper, and I would love to take you out some times and show you a good time. Is that possible?"

"Maybe..!" Nina said with a smile.

"What's your name?"

"Lisa."

"Please to meet you, did you just move around here or something?"

"Yes me and my sister. Her job just relocated out here, so I came out here to help her get situated."

"I see – well, I would love to be able to take you ladies out and show you around. Where are you staying at?"

"I'm staying at the Comfort Inn on Colorado Blvd. I caught the bus to the Aurora Mall and missed my bus so I started walking."

"Baby you ain't got to walk, can I give you a ride?"

"That would be nice, let me grab a soda o'kay."

"Sure baby, get what you want, I got you!"

Nina switched over to the soda box and grabbed a 7 Up and took it to the counter and grab some Big Red gum.

Paper's eyes was glued on her fine sexy ass all the way to the soda box and back, and gave the casher two dollars as the Asian man put the soda and gum in a small bag and gave Paper his change. "Come on baby." Paper said as they walked out of the store.

Red Rum saw Paper and Nina exist the store together and jumped in Paper's Range Rover, and Red Rum pulled off and headed for the motel as Itty Bitty said, "I told you!" They laughed with a scandalous look in their eyes.

Red Rum and Itty Bitty beat Paper and Nina to the motel, and they ran in and hid in the bathroom as they waited for Nina to get there with Paper.

Nina arrived five minutes after them and like always, she had her Vic caught up in her web of deception. She opened up the motel room door, and Paper was mackin' his ass off. He thought that he just stumbled across some fresh pussy from this fine ass Cubin dime piece. She said, "Have a set handsome." Paper sat down as he seen Red Rum and Itty Bitty running in full speed with guns drawn. Paper tried to go for his gun, but Red Rum had his 357 magnum in his face at point blank range.

Red Rum said, "Try it nigga, and I'll put your brains all over that muthafucken wall."

Paper raised his hands as Itty Bitty took Paper's 45 automatic out of the front of his belt, and put it in his pocket and said, "lay your punk ass down before I get mad nigga." Paper layed down as Itty Bitty helped him by dragging Paper down hard and handcuffed him behind his back.

Nina laughed with Red Rum as Itty Bitty showed off his brut force. Then Itty Bitty searched Paper and took his fat diamond ring, Jacob diamond face Movado watch, and a fat diamond iced out chain and bracelet to match. Then he took the wod of money that was in his pockets and started counting it.

Red rum said, "listen nigga, you can walk away from this shit unharmed, all we want is the money and dope."

"O'kay man, just don't kill me!" The money's in the duffle bag in the back seat of the truck."

Red Rum looked at Nina and said "go get it Boo." As he handed her Papers keys and she got up and walked out as Red Rum peeped out the crack of the curtain watching her back to make sure that she don't cause any suspicion.

Nina walked back in and put the duffle bag on the bed and Red Rum poured out the money and said, "nigga what's this?"

"Man that's all that I got..!"

"Listen nigga, we ain't got time to play with you, either you tell us where the money and dope is or we're gong to do you real bad!"

"Man, I don't have no more money, I was about to use that money to re-cope with."

"Yeah right nigga, …. Nina cut off the head of this nigga's dick. Red Rum said as Nina walked over to her purse and pulled out a long straight razor, and walked back over to Paper and started unbuckling his belt.

"Wait, Wait, man! I can get you some more money but you got to take me to my tilt. I'll give it all to you, just don't do me like that man." Paper pleaded.

"O'kay, where do you live at?"

"I got a house in Westminster!"

"Who lives there with you?"

"Nobody man, I live by myself."

"You know if you try anything stupid then I'm gonna kill you, but if you give me what I want, then you can live to hustle another day." Red Rum made it clear.

"Man, I'm not trippin off the money just don't kill me, ya'll can have it all…!"

"O'kay, now how do we get to your house?"

Paper told them the directions and they escorted him out, and Red Rum made him slide in the back seat of the

G-ride next to him while, Nina drove and Itty Bitty set in the passenger seat. They jumped on the freeway and Paper started to get real paranoid because he realized that they didn't care that he saw their faces.

"He said man, I ain't dumb! I know ya'll gonna kill me!"

"Nigga all we want is the money, we're not trippin off killing you!" Red Rum said in a calm tone to try to calm him down.

"You're lying, that's why you ain't tripping off me seeing ya'll faces." Paper said to support his claim.

"We don't care about you seeing our faces, we're not from out here and you'll never see us again. You're so dumb, you don't even know that someone close to you put us on you, but they said don't kill you, they just want half of the money that we're about to take from you."

Paper's mind started thinking and wondering, who could it be? Was one of the homies jealous of his shin that they would send some-out-of-town nigga's to take his bank? Maybe it's that nigga Cojo, he knows how much money a nigga's been clockin. Or maybe it's that punk bitch Cindy, still mad that I dumped her when she said she was pregnant. Whoever it is, they must be close if they didn't want me dead. Man, what should I do. Paper thought to himself.

"Listen nigga we will still torture the shit out of you, and even fuck you over bad if you don't give us the fuckin money. So make it light on yourself…!" Red Rum said as he pulled out a big buck knife.

"O'kay, O'kay, turn up ahead at the next corner, make a right and my address is 211.."

Nina slowed down at the address and Red Rum said, "do you got an alarm or anything like that?"

"Naw man, this is the good area here." Red Rum reached in Paper's pocket and pulled out his keys and said, "which one is it?"

"Those two!"

Red Rum gave them to Nina and said, "I want you both to go check it out, if he lied, then you know what to do. I'll keep Mr. Paper company until you get back. Mr. Paper if anything goes wrong, I'ma kill you without thinking twice. So you better hope no damn dogs jump-out and make a scene."

"I ain't got no damn dogs man."

"Good..!"

Nina and Itty Bitty went up to the door, opened it, and went in.

Paper said, "I told you, man! I ain't gonna lie to you.
I don't feel like dying today."

Red Rum said, "that's smart of you as he saw Nina
and Itty Bitty come out of the house and walk up and said,
"everything look's cool!"

Alright Paper, let's go get that money that you've been
stacking. Nina grabbed hold of Paper's left arm since he
was handcuffed from behind, and Red Rum grabbed him
by the back of his neck and shoved him along into the
house with Itty Bitty trailing close behind them.

Paper took them up stairs and opened-up the safe.
Itty Bitty started grinning when he saw all the money stack
in hundred dollar bills banded together, in four neat rolls.
Itty Bitty then grabbed a suit case that he saw laying near
by and used it to put all the cash and jewelry from the safe
into it.

Then he spotted an AK 47 sitting in the closet and put
on his brownies and picked it up. "Damn, I always
wanted one of these."

Red Rum smiled and said, "so tell me where's the
dope?"

"Man I don't got no dope here." Paper said trembling.

"I don't ask you that, I asked you <u>WHERE IS THE
DOPE?</u>"

Paper thought about it and knew that if he took them to the dope house then one of the young homies might be close around or Cojo and could help him. "Man Big Al keeps the dope in an apartment over on Federal Street.

Red Rum knew that he just trapped him up and said, "I heard of that name, ain't that the nigga you work for?"

Paper was really confused now, realizing that he didn't know who Big Al was but knew that his life depended on his worth. So he said, "Yeah, that's the nigga I work for, and basically he's the nigga that runs this town."

"Oh yeah, where do he live?"

"That I don't know, nobody knows."

"Nigga what, you take me for a fool or something, you mean to tell me that he let you pick up his money and have access to his stash house where he keeps his damn dope, but you don't know where he lives? You must think that I'm playing with you or something."

Paper looked at Nina who was sitting on the bed across from him and she flicked her straight razor opened. Paper said, "Wait a minute man, he makes me take the money over to his bitch's house, name Gwen, and she takes it to him."

"Well where do Gwen live?"

"She lives right around the way, about two miles from here."

"Who do she live with?"

"She lives by her self I think....! They must be kicking it on some sex shit or something."

"You take her his money, once you collect it?"

"Yeah."

"That's why you got access to the stash spot, because you deliver the dope to the workers and the buyers?"

"Exactly!"

"Well everything makes sense now, so that means that we need to go see Gwen then!"

Paper knew that he put his foot in his mouth on this one, but knew that he had to play along in hopes that he could buy some time, or find the right opportunity to make his get away. As long as he was alive then there was a chance of survival.

"Listen man, can you loosen these handcuff's a little bit?"

Red Rum laughed and said, "Itty Bitty, can you help the brother out?"

Itty Bitty walked over to him and socked him dead off in the eye, and dropped him to the floor. "That should take your mind off the pain of the handcuffs." And Red Rum, Nina, and Itty Bitty started bustin' up!

"Get up nigga, and let's roll...!" Red Rum said as he picked Paper up and walked him back out to the G-ride.

Ten minute later, they were knocking at Gwen's door.

"Who is it?" Gwen said as she walked up to the door in her pimped out two bedroom townhouse.

"It's Paper..!"

Gwen peeped out of the peep hole, and seen Paper standing there and opened up the door.

As the door opened, Red Rum pushed Paper through it real hard and pushed him and Gwen down to the floor as Red Rum and his crew stepped in with guns drown.

"What's going on?" Gwen screamed.

"Listen bitch, "Red Rum said as he pulled her by her hair and turned her around so he could hand cuff her.

Itty Bitty and Nina came from searching the townhouse for other people and said, "It's clear."

"O'kay Ms. Gwen, you have two choices, you can give us the money that we came for, that Big Al keeps here, or we can torture you and make you tell us! We just want the money, we didn't come here to hurt you unless you choose it."

"No, that ain't necessary." She said as she looked at Paper with disgust. It's up stairs in the closet, in the safe. The combination is 5 – 9- 11, and the dope is in the duffle bag next to it.

Red Rum eyes got big when she mentioned the dope, he gestured to Itty Bitty as he grinned and went to retrieve the money and dope.

Paper never considered the fact that Big Al would even be crazy enough to keep his dope and money together "Damn," he cursed to himself, this might fuck up his opportunity to make it to the next spot where the homies will be close by. Paper looked up at Red Rum and said, "You know, that it's another stash spot where Big Al keeps money and dope at on Federal Street."

Red rum smiled at the thought, knowing that Paper was trying to set him up to go on the dope street where all of his homeboys be hanging out at. "Is that right Red Rum said, "well, we might have to check it out when we leave here then." He gazed at Nina, as they both smiled.

"Mister," Gwen said as she looked up at Red Rum. "If your gonna kill us before you leave, just let me kill this soft ass pathetic nigga for you, or at least watch him die first."

Itty Bitty came down with the two duffle bags and said, "that's right baby, keep it gansta, I like her!"

Paper said, "Fuck that bitch 'Cuzz,' I don't give a damn about another nigga's money… my life means more to me then some crumbs."

"Ah shit blood, I know that this nigga didn't just smug us." Itty Bitty said as he put down the bags.

Paper's eyes got big when he realized that they was 'Bloods', he fucked up and knew it! "Wait man, I didn't mean it like that, she's my cousin man."

"I ain't his damn cousin, he's a Crip! Nigga don't bitch up now! I know that you was a buster when I first met you! Gwen said as she exposed him.

Nina went into the kitchen and came back with a big Jason knife, and looked at Red rum, as Red Rum shook his head 'yes,' and smiled.

Paper was arguing with Gwen and didn't even see it coming. Nina stuck the knife through his heart from in back, and his eyes got big as he strained to look up at Red Rum and let out his last breath.

"That's what your bitch ass gets nigga, and this ain't over, because I'ma expose your bitch ass in hell too!" Gwen said, as everybody started laughing.

"Listen Gwen, where do Big Al live?" Red Rum asked.

"I don't know Sir., I can't lie, if I did know, then I wouldn't tell you....so you might as well kill me too and get it over with."

Red Rum and his crew started busting up as Itty Bitty said, "Now that's a down bitch!"

"Listen Gwen, I respect your gangsta, and I'ma let you live today, and pray that we never cross path again. Tell Big Al that Crenshaw Mafia's will catch up with him soon, and when we do, then we're gonna do him worse then his buster ass comrade here. Go take her up stairs and tie her ass up." Itty Bitty grabbed Gwen and picked her up.

"Listen Sir., as far as I'm concerned, you and your crew had on ski masked, and I will never mention any of this to the police. That's my word and I thank you!" Red Rum shook his head and reached into the duffle bag and grabbed a kilo of cocaine and said, "This is for your realness, hide it for her so when she get's loose, she can hustle up on a new Escalade or something."

"Thank you, thank you so much!" Gwen said as Itty Bitty took Gwen up stairs and tied her ass up in the bathroom. And said, "Take care baby, and stay sucka free!"

"I will thank you!"

Itty Bitty walked back down stairs and saw that Red Rum cut off Paper's head, and set it on the table as if it was staring at the door. "Boy I don't know who's crazier, you or your crazy ass bitch."

Nina playfully hit Itty Bitty in the arm, and said, "I'm not the crazy one, you two are, but I think that ya'll wearing off on me!"

Red Rum washed off the knife and took it with him as they left out of the door.

They made it back to the apartment and counted the money as they watched the news, but it never showed the murder scene. They hit for $480, 000 thousand dollars and 8 birds. Red rum said, "Now that was a good lick!"

"Yeah, but I'm pissed that Gwen down ass stole my shin! That was a master piece." Nina said with a smile on her face as she looked at Itty Bitty.

Itty Bitty looked at Red Rum and said, "I told you that she was crazy!" and everyone busted up laughing.

Chapter 9
The Trigger Got No Heart

Sin, Big Boy, and G-Real pulled up to the liquor store on Broadway and went in to grab something to drink and some blunt papers, so they can get their little party cranked up with some young hoes that they met earlier at the South Glenn mall. They already rented the motel room with the Jacuzzi hook up and had nothing but sex on their minds.

"Listen ya'll," G-Real said as they were walking out. "We need to get a train going on them hoes tonight. You know how we do it."

"Fuck it man, we don't love them hoes!" Big Boy said as everyone laughed.

"Hey Sin?" A voice said as Jim Jim and little Willie stood off to the side with Blue bandanas tied over their faces. "Game over Bitch," Jim Jim said as he and little Willie started unloading their guns. Jim Jim had a Mac 10 and little Willie had two twin 357 magnums.

Sin looked up when he heard his name called, and him and this two homies G-Real and Big Boy turned, and saw death as Sin said, "Fuck you, Blood," and went for his 9mm as the bullets hit him hard and without mercy. All three of them laid in a puddle of blood as Jim Jim and little Willie laughed as they ran away.

* * * *

Keyona and Teyona was in their new G-ride, a 88 Comero Iroc that they just got so they could put down their next lick in. They both had on dark blue khaki suits, dark blue base ball caps with their hair tucked in it, and big dark sun glasses to hide their appearance. Teyona had two gloc 9mm and Keyona had her Desert Eagle 44 and 3.80 automatic. They we're driving around on the prowl, when they seen Cojo in his fixed up 1986 Chevy Caprice, with the light blue candy paint, sitting on 24 inch Chrome rims and bumping his sound with two of his homeboys.

Teyona said, "Pull up on side of him!"

"Let just follow him and see if we can catch him slipping some where." Keyona said as she tried to debate the issue.

"Fuck that, he might get away! Just pull up on side of him, and I'm gonna blow his damn head off."

Cojo pulled up at the red light on Colorado Blvd as he instinctively gazed over at the car pulling up on side of him from his mirror, and he seen some niggas in an old school Camaro coming up on side of him. He looked to the side as he seen a hand come out of the window holding a gun and ducked his head as he said, "watch out…!"

Keyona pulled up on Cojo and Teyona reached out of her window as Cojo ducked, and Teyona started shooting at the niggas that was in her sight. She shot seven times before Keyona punched off and ran the red light. Teyona looked up and kept on bussin as the car shot forward. She emptied the rest of the bullets into the side, front, and wind shield of Cojo Caprice. Cojo rose up with his 45 automatic as the Camaro was driving off, and he started bussin at the back of the Camaro, shattering the back window and knocking out the back tail lights.

Teyona said, "Damn, I missed that nigga! Are you alright, Key Key?"

"Yeah, I'm cool…!" Keyona said as he looked into her rear view mirror with her feet to the floor of the gas peddle.

Cojo looked over at Sparks who was tilted over died with his brains scattered on the passenger window, and then at Crime who was in the back seat, and Crime said, "get them nigga cuzz," and Cojo punched out giving chase after the Camaro.

Keyona said, "We got company and hit a corner," as Teyona reloaded her 9mm and jumped into the back seat.

The Caprice hit the corner a couple of seconds after Keyona and Teyona said, "Slow this car down..!"

When Cojo punched out after the twins, Detective Jones and his partner Robert Price was across the street about to make a left turn, as they saw the shoot out take place. They were in a unmark new Crown Victoria, and ducked down as they saw Cojo start shooting back. After Cojo took off after the Camaro the detective busted a u-turn and went in hot pursuit of them both. Detective Price was on his CB radio calling for back up.

Keyona slowed down after she hit another corner, and when Cojo turned the corner the Camaro was right there waiting and Cojo slammed on his breaks as Teyona started unloading both of her 9mm into his windshield Cojo tried to duck but the bullets caught him in the shoulder before he was able to fully duck. "Damn, I'm hit!" He said as he reached up with his 45 automatic and started bussin through his front windshield.

Crime was busting his 9mm too, and Keyona punched back off before the bullets of their gun could fully do any damage. Cojo tried to punch back out after them, but his radiator was hit, and his car died as steam came smoking out from beneath the hood of his car. He saw the police car rolled up and stop behind him, 30 feet away.

Cojo jumped out and started bussin' at the cops. The first two shots hit Detective Price in the head and dropped him dead and Cojo jumped behind a car just as Detective Jones returned fire and barely missed him. Crime tried to jump out of the car bussin, but he tripped as he was getting out, because he had to come out from the back seat, and his foot got caught-up in the seat belt. Crime jumped backed on his feet as Detective Jones had him in dead sight, and hit him five times in the stomach and chest area.

Cojo reloaded as he saw his homeboy get gun down, so he jumped up bussin, as he exchanged shots with Detective Jones tic for tac.

Detective Jones jumped up to meet his advancement head on, and got hit in the left shoulder and bullets lodge into his bullets-proof vest, as he hit Cojo six times in the chest and dropped him dead.

Detective Jones looked over at his dead partner who was laid out leaking blood from his head, Detective Jones anger rose, as he kicked a dent in the back finder of the police vehicle. Other police officer came pulling up and running over to him.

* * * *

The twins pulled up in an alley where they parked their rent a car and set the Camaro on fire as they jogged away. As they were jogging away from the car on fire they seen a base head run out, and say, "Hey you're gonna burn down the whole damn neighborhood."

Teyona turned around and pointed her gun at his face as Keyona said, "NO," and grabbed her arm and said, "come on let's go." Teyona looked at her as they turned and ran away.

They jogged to the rent a car that was parked near by and jumped inside. Teyona started taking off her disguise, and when Keyona got four blocks away, she took off her disguise too, and then jumped on the freeway as they went to get rid of the evidence, and then went home to wash away their sins.

Teyona turned on the TV and the shoot out was all over the news. The news caster said that it was another gang related incident. They mentioned how the police saw it go down, and followed the suspects in hot pursuit, and how the gang suspects who were involved in the shot out turned their guns on the two detectives as they made it to the scene. They said that the shoot out that occurred with the police and gang members, resulted in one detective getting killed and all three gang members died at the scene as well. Two of them died from the detective return fire and the third one as a result of the previous shot out with the other gang members. They mentioned that Detective Jones a drug enforcement officer was the officer who killed the two gang members, after one of the gang member killed his partner.

Then they showed the scene with the Camaro burned up, and said that, when the police arrived they caught a man trying to put out the fire, and they flashed the camera on the old base head as he was talking to Detective Jones.

Teyona said, "I knew that I should've killed that muthafucka....look at him he's telling it all." Then she looked at Keyona, with a I told you so look on her face.

"Tey, Tey, he ain't seen nothing, we had on disguise, so he can't pen point us."

"I'm just saying, we can't be slipping like that," Teyona shouted!

"Tey, Tey, we ain't no damn cold hearted killers, we're just getting revenge on the ones who was involved with daddy's and Lala's murder, that's all!"

Just then Teyona's cell phone rang and she walked over to answer it.

"Hello."

"Hey young tender, how are my two young angels doing?"

Teyona recognized Red Rum voice and said, "Is this uncle Red?"

"The one and only."

She smiled and said, "We're doing fine Unc!"

"Good, good, I'm watching your dance video and I'm loving your work. Ya'll dance just like your father and you know that he had moves."

Teyona laughed as Keyona said, "Tell him that I said hi."

"Tell her that I send mine, and my family do too, especially the baby face one!" They started laughing.

Teyona said, "Did you ever go dancing with my father?"

"Oh yeah, on a couple occasions, and he was a damn fool too.... my type of nigga!"

They shared a good laugh. "Listen up young tender, you ain't got to worry about that Paper no more, we've took care of that debt for you. And we made a good profit too, do you ladies need some ends?"

"No, we're cool, and thank you for paying that debt off for us, we appreciate it!"

"Our pleasure baby, that's what family is for…don't worry we'll be around for a minute, just wanted to keep you posted, and check on you, if you need me, then holla o'kay?"

"O'kay."

"Bye, bye, young tender."

"Bye," Teyona said as they hung up.

She looked over at Keyona and said "Key Key, they got Paper for us. He said that they took his money too!"

"I knew that they were putting in work, they just be doing it real slick. I think that they're trying to rob them niggas too….you know, come up a little while they're doing their thang."

"Shit, I wouldn't put it pass them!" Teyona said.

"Listen Tey Tey, that's almost everybody except Big Al, so when we get him, then we can leave this state and nightmare behind us."

"I agree!" Teyona said as they smiled at each other. I'ma call G-Mom and let her know that we'll be ready to leave real soon. I know that she's probably worrying herself crazy." And they started laughed at the thought of it.

Chapter 10
Ghetto Breed and Ghetto Conscious

The twins were taking care of their business making sure that all of their father's and Lala stuff was in storage, and the furniture and the rest of the stuff they were donating it to Goodwill. They were at their old house when the people from Goodwill was emptying out the rest of the furniture from the house putting it on their truck, just then the twins saw an undercover police car pull up. Teyona stood back and gave her 3.80 automatic to Keyona, as Keyona walked into the house and stashed both of their guns in the secret department under the bathroom sink. Keyona walked back out as Detective Jones walked up and said, "Hello Ms. Fox, I'd like to ask you both to come down to the station with me...! There is some questions that I'd like to ask you!"

"Pertaining to what?" Teyona asked.

"It's better if we discuss this matter downtown."

"Sir, are you placing us under arrest for something? Teyona questioned.

"No I'm detaining you." He said, as two police cruisers pulled up.

Teyona looked over at Keyona, and said don't say anything, request to call our attorney!"

Keyona shook her head yes, as she locked the door to the house, and the police officers that pulled up separated them in different cars, and took them downtown to the police station.

Once downtown at the police station Detective Jones separated them in different interrogation rooms, and went to go speak to them.

He spoke to Teyona first, and as he walked into the interrogation room he said, "Ms. Fox, you are in some hot water!"

Teyona eyes deemed as she looked at him trying to read his face and body language.

Your sister is in the other room telling it all…! I'm gonna give you an opportunity to come clean just this one time, before I let the District Attorney take advantage of you. Now I can help you, but you got to come clean now, or it's out of my hands."

"Mr. Jones, I don't know what you're talking about, and I would like my phone call so I can call my attorney. I do have a right to have my attorney present, and I would like to exercise that right now!"

"Well being that you're not under arrest means that, that right, that you are trying to request 'you are not entitled to!" You're just being held for questioning."

"Either or, I still have my rights, and I WANT MY ATTORNEY PRESENT...!" Teyona said with authority.

"You think that you're so smart don't you, we got an eye witness who said that he seen you at the scene of a crime lighting a fire to a car that was involved in a murder. Now either you come clean now, and save your little pretty ass, or I'm going to make sure that you face the death penalty."

"Sir., you obviously got me confused with somebody else, because I don't know what the hell you're talking about. Now give me my phone call so I can call my attorney, or arrest me so I can exercise my damn rights."

"You think that you're so smart, but the smart ones always end up loosing, just like your father."

Teyona looked him in dead in his blue eyes and spit right in his face, and said, "That's for my father you race ass son-of-a-bitch!"

Detective Jones turned fire engine red, as someone knocked on the double glass window and he stormed out.

"Listen Ms. Fox, your sister Teyona told us everything, and said that it was all your idea and you made her participate."

"Keyona started busting up."

"Oh, you think it's funny, how funny do you think that it's going to be, when your ass is facing the death penalty. Stop laughing! What's so damn funny? Detective Jones hollered.

Keyona looked at him and said, "you are! Listen, I want to speak to my attorney now!"

"We got a key witness!"

Keyona started singing….!

"Stop singing! Stop Singing I said..!" With that Detective Jones walked out on fire as Keyona started laughing again.

The police throw them both in a jail cell together to try to break them. They wouldn't give them a phone call or nothing. The police came around with dinner and Teyona said, "We're not eating, we're on a hunger strike and we want to call our attorney!"

The deputy said, "I'll tell the lieutenant that you both decline to eat."

"That's right baby-go hard!" An old dark skin lady said who was two cells away.

Twenty minutes later a deputy brung a young white girl to the cell, and put her in the cell with the twins. The twins learned sign language as little girls, and knew how to speak it fluently. Their father made them learn it and Lala too, and some day's he'll make everyone in the house speak sign language all through the day. So the girls was two of a kind with it.

The white girl walked over to them and said, "Hi, I'm Linda! You must be the two girls that they were talking about. Ya'll had a shoot out with some gang members or something, didn't you?"

Teyona looked at Keyona and they both smiled, as Teyona jumped up and started beating up on Linda, and Keyona jumped in and assisted with given Linda a ghetto ass whoop'in. Then Linda started screaming for help as Teyona ripped off her shirt, and they saw a microphone that she had taped between her breast. Linda, jumped up off the ground, and ran to the bars as the twins was on her ass given her a gangsta ass kickin'.

The deputies said, "Get off of her, get off of her ya'll," and they ran in as Keyona and Teyona rushed them and started fighting them as they ran into the cell. Three more male deputies ran in the cell, and wrestled the twins down and handcuffed them. Teyona seen a police on top of her sister's back holding her down, and she pulled her leg back, and kicked the young white male deputy right in the face, and sent him flying off of Keyona, and knocked him half unconscious.

"Grab her damn legs, both of them." The deputy said as they hog tied the twins and carried them both to different single cells.

"Don't talk to nobody Keyona." Teyona said as they were carried away.

It was 3:00a.m. that morning, when Teyona's cell door opened. She was laying down with one arm handcuffed to the bunk. Teyona jumped up and saw a light skin black female deputy walk in. She held her finger over her lips, telling Teyona to be quiet and said, "I'm a good friend of Lala's she use to curl my hair at your beauty salon. Listen, they don't have anything on you girls, Detective Jones is just assuming about you two because some nigga said, 'two people wearing disguises ran from the scene, after a car was burned that was used in a shoot out'. It was said, that the witness said, 'that one of the persons wearing the disguise had a voice of a female, so he's assuming that both the person's running away from the scene were females. Then the lady deputy's eyes got big, as to jester and expression like 'what the fuck is that, go figure!' "I used to look out for Lala on things that your father was interested in knowing. You feel me?"

Teyona just shook her head yes!

"That girl that they put in the cell with ya'll was their only chance and long shot. They got to let you go within 72 hours, or come up with some type of charges so that they can hold you, understand?"

"Yes."

"They violated all of your rights, and if you got an attorney, then let me know and I'll call him for you, if not, then I'll try to find one or call someone who could help."

"My attorney's name is Robert Parker he's in the book." Teyona said.

"Good I'll get right on it, here I brung you a snickers… give me the wrapper and I'll get rid of it for you. Do you want me to tell your sister anything?"

"Just tell her that you're going to contact our attorney for us, and he'll be here tomorrow."

"O'kay baby! Ya'll be careful too, because it's a vicious blood bath going on with the Crips and Bloods out there in the streets and gang members is dying by the numbers. At least, three to six bodies a day. So be careful, and don't trust no one! Take care Baby." The police deputy said as she loosened the handcuff so Teyona can slip in and out of it, then smiled and walked out. Teyona thought about how the lady just risked her job to give her a heads up on what was happening and she thought about Lala watching over them, and smiled as she ate the candy bar.

At 8:30a.m. that morning, Attorney Parker was at the Denver police department causing all kinds of hell. He asked to see the Captain in charge and threaten to call the Mayor if the Captain didn't come to speak with him. The lieutenant knew that the shit was about to hit the fan, and didn't want his name mentioned in it, so he called Captain Davis who was having his breakfast, and told him that an attorney was there requesting to see him, or he was threatening to call the Mayor. The Captain threw his toast back onto his plate and went down to see what the fuss was all about.

When the Captain arrived Attorney Parker asked to see the arrest warrant for the girls. The Captain wasn't aware of the arrest, and tried to pull up the information on the girls, but he couldn't fine anything. He looked at the inmate detainment roster, and saw the girls on it, and saw that Detective Jones was the one who detain them.

Attorney Parker requested to know what probable cause did they have to detain the girls, and requested to speak to them. The Captain didn't know, so he escorted Attorney Parker to an interview room, and told the deputy to bring the girls to the room so they could speak with their attorney.

Jamie, the deputy who made the call for the twins smiled as she went to get the girls. She opened up Teyona's cell door and said, "Ms. Fox, your attorney is here to see you!" Then she went over and handcuffed her behind her back and told the other deputy to take Teyona to the interview room while she goes and get her sister. Teyona looked at Jamie, and Jamie cracked a small smile, as the other older female deputy escorted Teyona to the interview room.

When Teyona make it to the interview room, the Captain was there with Attorney Parker. Teyona had a scratch on her face, and bruises on her arm, back, and legs. When she saw her attorney she said, "they told me that I didn't have a right to have you present, and wouldn't let me make a phone call. I told him that I wanted my attorney, but he said that I had 'No Rights', then they hit me and my sister, and hog tied us, and handcuffed us to the bed all night."

"Who did this to you?" The Captain said in shock!

"Detective Jones and the other deputies that was on duty yesterday."

"What?"

"Yes, look at all the bruised on my arms, and my back hurt's and they beat my legs."

The Captain and Attorney looked at her back and arms as Keyona was escorted in by Jamie.

"This is absurd!" The Captain said.

"No this is police brutality, unconstitutional, and a damn disgrace to justice." Attorney Parker stated.

"Deputy Grant, take off these girls handcuffs", and the Captain looked at the lieutenant and said, "get me Detective Jones here now!"

"Yes Sir!" And the lieutenant hurried out.

After Jamie took off the handcuffs she walked out. The Captain said, "Attorney Parker I can assure you that I'll get to the bottom of this immediately." He looked at Keyona's wrists and hands, and they were swollen, he then stormed out and shut the door.

"Are you alright?" Attorney Parker asked Keyona.

"No, they beat us up!"

"Don't worry, they will pay for that I assure you that, now what happened?"

Teyona told him how they got detained, and how she requested to have their attorney present, and the detective told her that she didn't have any Rights to an attorney. He said, that he was gonna try to give her the death penalty if she didn't admit to a crime that she didn't know anything about. Then she explained how he put a undercover cop in the cell with them wearing a wirer, and she got mad because they wouldn't talk to her, so then she swung at her, and they started fighting. That's when the police ran in the cell and started beating them up, and took them in different cells, and handcuffed them to the bed. Teyona went on to explain how Detective Jones rubbed on her pussy when the other police left the cell, and said that he was going to come back and fuck her while she was hand cuffed to the bed, and she was scared all night and couldn't sleep.

Attorney Parker's face turned red with anger, as he heard what happened. Keyona knew that Teyona made up the part about her being molested, but knew that Detective Jones must've been left in the cell with her, after they handcuffed her to the bed, and the other police officers left out, so it had to be the perfect opportunity for him to do so.

Keyona told their attorney how she requested her attorney present, and was denied her Rights, and how she was threaten to admit to a crime that she didn't know about, and then, how they assaulted her and handcuffed her to the bed. The attorney took out his cell phone, and took pictures of the girls' bruises. Then he called the Mayor who he plays golf with and knows personally, while he was still sitting there in the interview room with the girls.

Teyona looked over at Keyona and smiled. And said, "are you alright Key Key?"

"Yeah, I'm fine Tey Tey, what about you?"

"I'm o'kay too, whatever happens just don't trust no one o'kay? And remember that I love you so much!" Teyona whispered as Keyona smiled and shook her head.

Detective Jones was at a murder scene that happened about five o'clock that morning, when he received a phone call from the station. He was standing by a Lincoln Navigator on 24 inch chrome rims, that had three gang members in it shot to death, and another body was twisted-up near the back of the truck where the gas tank was. Apparently two rival gang members caught them slipping at the gas station early in the morning. The three men inside of the truck got hit with an AK 47 riffle, and the one in the back of the truck, got hit four times with a Desert Eagle 44. It was a horrible sight to see, but a sight that was becoming all too common.

Detective Jones hung up his phone and said, "Damn," as he went and jumped in his unmarked police vehicle and headed for the station. He thought to himself that the murder rules out the Twins as suspects. "Damn!" He mumbled to himself.

The Captain received a call from the Mayor, and it wasn't a good sign. His job was threatened and he didn't like that one bit. Somebody was going to take the fall, and it wasn't going to be him. Detective Jones made it back to the station and the Captain and Lieutenant Smith of homicide was in the Captain's office waiting for him. Detective Jones stepped in and closed the door. The captain shouted, "Who gave you permission to detain those two girls?"

"Captain I was playing a hunch!"

"A hunch! What evidence do you have to come up with a hunch about them?"

"Well Captain, the man who was trying to put out the fire on the car that was used in the shoot-out that shot and killed my partner, he said, 'that one of the persons who started the fire sounded like a women'!"

"Didn't he also say that they had on disguises? And that he couldn't recognize them, and that they looked like men!"

"Yes, he said that too, but I figured that they could be the missing pieces to our puzzle, their father and step mother got killed by gang members, so they might be trying to seek revenge!"

"Detective all that you have given me so far is assumptions. Can you tell me what concrete evidence that you have against these two ladies to make you violate their entire god given constitutional rights?"

"Well Sir, we didn't come up with any evidence yet!"

"Well Detective, can you tell me what Judge authorized the use of a wire that you placed on that poor girl who's in the hospital now, and what authority did you go to that gave you permission to violated those ladies right?"

"I did it on my own Sir...!"

"You mean that you jeopardized the integrity of this department, by violating the chain of command, and rights of the innocent citizens of this state, on some Rambo shit?"

"Sir, it's a blood bath going on in them streets, and everybody is just sitting around watching."

"Detective if you wanted to play the role of a politician, then you should have run for Mayor or Governor! You've jeopardized the honor and integrity of this department, and also this state, and I'm not going to tolerate that type of behavior out of my officers. Give me your badge and service pistol, you're on suspension with no pay pending investigation and possible prosecution."

"Possible prosecution, how so?"

"I'll tell you how so, because the girls that you've choose to violate their constitutional rights, said that you and other officers from this department beat them, and one of them alleged that you molested her and threaten to rape her."

"Captain she's lying, I didn't beat her, molest her or threaten to rape her… that's absurd!"

"I'll tell you what's absurd, the way you disrespected this department, and took it upon yourself to play judge and prosecutor. Now hand over your damn badge and service pistol, and you can clean out your desk on your way out! Be happy that I don't have you arrested and locked-up pending investigation. I advise you to stay out of the way, and do some praying!" The Captain took his badge and gun and he shook his head and walked out.

The twins was immediately released and informed of the investigation into the allege officer abuse, and misconduct allegation. The girls thanked their attorney, and he said that he would be filing a multi-million dollar law suit against the state, police department, and officers in charged. He dropped the girls back off at the old house, and told them to be careful, and if they needed anything then just call. The girls thank him again and they departed.

The twins grabbed their guns and jumped back to the stash house. They showered and jumped in their Corvette and went to get their hair and nails done. After that, they called up Red Rum and asked him to meet them at the Aurora Mall on the bottom parking level. Red Rum arrived with his crew in a black Tahoe Truck with tinted windows, but it was still stocked. They embraced each other, and thought that it might be best to talk inside the truck.

The girls told him everything that happened with them getting detained, and all of the good information that they found out. Red Rum and his crew was glad to hear that their plan and efforts is having such a powerful effect.

Red Rum offered to finish Big Al off for the girls, so the girls could leave and go on with their life. But the twins decline to accept his offer, Teyona said that they couldn't rest until Big Al was in the grave, and they wanted to be the one to kill him. The twins told Red Rum to leave and they could handle it from here, and he said that he would go when the times right. They hugged and kissed and departed. It was no question that a deep bound was made between them all.

The twins went into the mall and bought some clothes and desired accessories, and left. They went back to the stash house, and got some rest as they cuddled up and talked the night away like little girls having a slumber party.

Chapter 11
Who Can You Trust?

Big Al was at his new safe house, with his two new lieutenants Jim Jim and Little Willie, as he was cooking up five kilo's and sacking them all up. He moved his safe house after Gwen told him how Paper sold him out, and told the robbers were Big Al's other stash spot was located. Big Al was so pissed that he had Jim Jim throw Paper's head and body in the Crest Creek Reservoir. He also relocated Gwen and give her 20 g's to go shopping with, for her realness and the troubles that she endured. Gwen really liked Big Al, but he just considered her some pussy that he kept on the side, and had no intentions of allowing her to become anything more then just that. After the robbery occurred, Gwen was thinking about packing her personal stuff up and leaving, but Big Al paid for her rent and car note to her new Cadillac Escalade, so she thought that it might be in her best interest to stick around a little longer, and stack her money so when she did leave, she'll have a nice amount of money put to the side. She knew that Big Al trusted her a lot, and counted on her to pick up his money from his two lieutenants, and to hold his dope.

After the robbery happened, Big Al made his lieutenants call Gwen up, and had it to were, Gwen would have to meet them to pick up the money and then she would call Big Al, and Big Al would go pick up the money at her house. She was paid a thousand dollars a week along with her bills being paid, so how could she complain. The only thing was that she couldn't fuck with any other niggas, it was like Big Al was the only dick that she could enjoy, and that wasn't much for her to be happy about. Nevertheless, it was something that she was willing to live with, especially considering the good financial benefits that it offered.

Gwen called Big Al, while Big Al was at his new stash spot with his new lieutenants cooking up the dope.

"Hello!" Big Al said as he answered his cell phone.

"Hi Al." Gwen said as she layed in her bed with her finger in her hot wet love box.

"Oh, what's up baby, what are you doing? Is everything alright?" Big Al asked.

"Yes, I was just laying here all hot and wet just thinking about you, and wondering was you coming by tonight?"

"Bitch you called me for that...! Don't ever call me and ask me am I coming over to fuck! I don't cater to no damn pussy, bitch – pussy cater to me! When I want some of your pussy, then I'll come by and fuck, but until then, you better use that damn dildo.   Do you hear me bitch?"

"Yeah." Gwen mumbled.

"What?"

"I said yeah!"

"Bitch you better sensor your damn tone when you talk to me, before I kick your wanna-be tuff ass. Now take a cold shower!" Big Al laughed and hung up.

"What's up cuzz, is everything cool?" Jim Jim asked.

"Yeah man, this bitch Gwen is just laying up horny and jockin a nigga for some dick, you know that I got to keep these bitches on a dick diet, so they won't get to damn possessive." Big said as they all laughed and Jim Jim pager went off.

"O'kay, this is that nigga Flip, he wants nine of these thangs." Jim Jim said as he read the code that Flip put in the beeper.

"Listen, tell these niggas that the price just went back up to eleven hundred dollars. I got to make up for these loses, and all this money that I'm spending on given my homeboy's who fall victim to this war a nice funerals. You feel me? Them nigga's just got to cut their rocks smaller."

"I feel you Big Al, and I'll let these nigga's know." Jim Jim said as he called Flip and set up the transaction. Then grab the nine ounces and rushed out the door.

Little Willie and Big Al stayed and finished cooking the dope up.

After Big Al hung up the phone with Gwen, she was pissed off. "How in the fuck is he just going to disrespect me like I'm just some stupid little hood rat of his? I almost lost my damn life protecting his punk ass. He must got me fucked up!" She said to herself as she layed in the bed but naked horny and now mad. She walked over and grabbed her rabbit ear dildo and said, "well I guess that it's me and you," as she cut it on and realized that the batteries was dead. "Damn, if it ain't one thang it's another." She said as she went down stairs in the kitchen to look for the new pack of batteries that she brought a while back. Her phone rang, and she slammed the kitchen draw and went to go answer it.

"Hello!

"Oh, what's up Jim Jim! "

"Yes, I guess I can meet you."

"Where are you?"

"Room 69, O'kay, I'll be there in fifteen minutes."

"Bye!"

"Damn, now I got to go pick up this nigga's money, this nigga is starting to get on my last nerves." Gwen said as she went up stairs and threw on her sun dress and grabbed her purse and left out.

* * * *

Big Al and Little Willie got through cooking up and sacking up the dope, they had to go over to the dope street and deliver 20 ounces to their workers and collect the money that the workers owed to Big Al for their last sack. They were in Little Willie's new Mustang as they pulled up, and the street was poppin as usual. All of the worker walked up to Big Al and Little Willie, and greeted them with their secret hand shake.

"What's up cuzz!" Loc said as he handed Little Willie $1900 hundred dollars.

"Right..!" Little Willie said as he counted the money. "Listen here Loc…these prices just went back up to $1100 hundred an ounce. Big Al took a major lose, and been making sure that all of his homeboy's get a decent burial, so we have to add in our loses. Just start cutting your rocks smaller.

"I feel you cuzz, I ain't trippin as long as our homeboy's get laid right, then I'm cool with it. I'ma make my money anyway, you feel me?"

"That's right young nigga, I feel you." Little Willie said as he gave Loc two ounces. Loc walked over to the base head's house to cut up his dope.

Little Willie loved the power and authority that he gained by being one of big Al's lieutenants and represented it to the fullest. He knew that a lot of his homeboy's was jealous of him but they knew that he was a gangsta, so they kept their thoughts and feelings to themselves. Little Willie collected all the money owed, and gave all of the worker's their sacks, as Big Al just stood around and conversed with all of his homeboy's who was standing around and coming through. This was his dope street and everyone knew it, and gave honor to his presents.

* * * *

Gwen made it to the Travel Lodge Motel fifteen minutes after Jim Jim called her. She went up to room 69, and knocked on the door. Jim Jim looked out through the peep hole and seen it was Gwen and opened the door.

"Hey baby, how you doing?"

"I'm doing fine!'

"Damn baby, you're looking sexy in that sun dress, showing off them big pretty legs. You got a brother feeling all horny and stuff."

"Boy you better stop before you get us in trouble." Gwen said as she blushed.

"Baby I don't kiss and tell, you know a brother got a major crush on your fine ass anyway." Jim Jim walked up and pulled Gwen close to him and started kissing her. Gwen's pussy was on fire, and he knew that she would give him some if he made the first move. Gwen was a cute honey coated sister who stood 5' 10" with a big butt and small chest that was a nice mouth full. She had a short hair style that brung out her pretty features, and her only down fall is that she was infatuated with the gangsta type of dope dealer niggas, and the money that they made. Jim Jim was her every desire for companionship, he was 6' 3" with a nice slim muscular built, dark brown skin with a nice sexy bald head, and a handsome smile to go with his thugged out appearance.

Jim Jim reached under Gwen's sun dress and squeezed her fat ass, as he notice that she wasn't wearing any panties. "I see that you was thinking about me!" She moaned.

"You're going to get us killed." Gwen whispered as she looked up in Jim Jim's eyes.

"Not if we have the same interest and desired." Jim Jim said as he pulled Gwen's sun dress over her head and gazed at her sexiness. "I wanted you from the first moment that I met you." He whispered as he layed her on the bed and took off his clothes, and fucked her like she ain't never been fucked before.

* * * *

"Big Al", - Little Willie said as he pulled him to the side. "I need to go get 18 more ounces from the stash spot. You want to roll with me?"

"Naw you go ahead….me, Rider, and Slim is about to run to the store and grab some drinks. We'll meet you back here."

"O'kay cool, I'll be back in ten minutes and I'ma put this money in the stash spot until I sell these other ounces, and then I'll holla at Gwen, or you can take it with you when you leave!"

"We'll see, just keep your eyes open!" Big Al said as Little Willie gave him their secret hand shake and left.

"Big Al said come on Slim let's roll out," then Big Al jumped into the passenger side of Slim's old school dark blue 96 Cadillac Seville SLS, and Rider jumped in the back seat as they left. They pulled up to the liquor store parking lot and parked as a big 67 Lincoln Continental drove into the parking lot right after them and ran full speed into the driver side of Slim's Cadillac door.

Slim said, "Watch out," as he ducked down diving into Big Al's lap, as the big Lincoln Continental reversed and came back straight for them at full speed.

The impact knocked the Cadillac flying ten feet away from where it was originally parked. Big Al opened up the passenger door, and jumped out with his big 44 Desert Eagle in his hand and started bussin at the nigga's who was jumping out of the Lincoln shooting back. Big Al pulled Slim out of the passenger side door onto the ground as Rider pushed the front seat up and bussed out of the driver side window hitting Little Man in the chest and dropping him to the ground.

Domu's Tec 9 was eating up the inside and the passenger side door of Slim's Cadillac. Slim and Rider ducked down as low to the ground as they could. Big Al ducked and ran for cover behind another parked car ten feet away, and the Tec 9 hit him in the butt right before he dove. Big Al hollered as he rolled for cover and felt his ass cheek on fire.

Stone had his 12 gauge automatic pump held high as he was creeping around the back of the Cadillac to get Slim and Rider and as soon as he got almost close enough, Domu clip ran out of bullets to his Tec 9, and he dropped the clip and started reloading, as Slim said, "Oh shit cuzz", then he saw Stone pointing his 12 gauge at him over the trunk of the Cadillac, and they both shot as the same time. The 12 gauge ripped off Slim's face, and Slim's 9mm hit Stone in the shoulder, and knocked him back, as Rider shot him five more times in his chest with his 9mm dropping him to the ground, dead!

Little Man was laying on the ground with his chest leaking and saw Rider laying on his back on the other side of the Cadillac, so he unloaded his 357 magnum into Rader's side.

Rider saw Stone fall to the ground after he shot him and said, "Fuck you cuzz!" As he felt the bullets from Little Man's 357 magnum penetrate his side, eating away his flesh.

Domu looked over at Big Al and Big Al shot two shots at him. Domu bussed a round of shots back at him as he tried to make an advancement toward where Big Al was hiding.

Tic and Creep was down the street at the hamburger joint as they saw Slim's Cadillac pass by and pull into the liquor store, and then they heard the gun shots begin and ran and jumped into their bucket and drove down to the liquor store. They came through the back alley way and seen the Lincoln smashed into Slim's Cadillac and they jumped out while Domu's back was turned, as he concentrated on getting at Big Al. Tic and Creep snuck up and caught Domu slipping as they gunned him down from behind.

Little Man raised his 357 magnum as he saw Creep running up shooting at Domu, but Little Man was out of bullets, as Creep looked at him and said, "you almost caught the Creepster slippin cuzz, but almost ain't good enough" and he unloaded the rest of his Gloc into Little Man's face.

They ran over and saw Rider and Slim dead and Big Al limped out from behind and they ran over and carried him with their shoulders back to their bucket, as they heard the police sirens coming closer and closer they punched out and took Big Al over to Ms. Robinson house, and Big Al paid her to attend to is wound.

The bullet went in and out of his butt cheek, so Ms. Robinson just cleaned, and sowed it up and put two gulls on it. Big Al gave Ms. Robinson $3,500 hundred dollars and they both were grateful.

Tic and Creep both received a-half a-bird a-piece, and they were glad to be at the right place at the right time.

* * * *

Jim Jim and Gwen was laying in each other's arms after enjoying two hours worth of the bom sex.

"So where do we go from here baby?" Jim Jim asked.

"Where do you want to go?"

"I don't care where I go, as long as I can have you by my side!" Jim Jim boldly said as he gazed deep into her pretty eyes.

"Do you mean that?"

"Of course I mean it baby....I'm loving your style and I need a thorough woman like you in my life."

"You know if Big Al finds out, we're dead!"

"Baby this world is bigger then Denver, we got the whole world to choose from. Just let me get my paper right, and we can go some where and start a new. Would you like that?"

"I would love that! I just got to know that your feelings is true and real for me."

"Baby every king deserves a queen, and you're the Queen that I desire, but I must ask you…am I the king that you choose?"

"Baby as long as you treat me right, I'll give you my all, and everything you desire." Gwen said as she gazed into his brown eyes.

"So do you choose me?"

"Yes, I do!"

Jim Jim gave her a passionate kiss. "Then it's us against the world. 'But listen,' I'ma be real with you! This shit is getting real ugly out here, and nigga's is dying by the car loads. So if we're going to roll out, then let's do it right. I don't play sucka or boy to know nigga. I'm just waiting for the right opportunity and then, I'm taking this nigga's shit and I'm out…!"

We can leave now, we ain't got to wait! I got like a hundred and something g's of his put up. We can take that and start a new life together anywhere." Gwen said with excitement in her voice.

"That sounds like a plan, give me a couple of days to get my shit right and we're out of here, but on my call, so get your shit together so when I call you then we can be gone within that hour. You feel me?"

"Yes, yes, I feel you baby – but where are we going?"

"I got some peoples in Memphis, we can go their and see how we like it, and if we don't like it, then we'll keep moving until we find some where that we like."

"What if he suspects us?" Gwen asked in a paranoid voice.

"Then I'll smoke his ass, and we'll get ghost."

"That's right! You're the type of man that I've dreamed of."

"You're my deepest desire Princess! Just keep your game tight, and if he comes through before we leave, and want some of that bom pussy, then let him get his rocks off, but remember who's woman you are now!"

"I will baby!" Gwen said as she kissed is neck.

"Now let's roll out, before I be here all night enjoying that bom lovin' that you got."

"It's yours now, so you can have it when-ever or where-ever you desire it at!"

"Yeah, we got to hurry up and roll out of here!"

"Just say the word and I'll be waiting for you!" Gwen said with a sexy smile.

"That's what I want to hear!" Jim Jim said as he kissed Gwen and then they got up and took a shower together and left.

Chapter 12
Your Enemy Is My Enemy!

The twins decided to kick back for a couple of days and get their business affairs in order. They gave Kim who manage the beauty salon twenty percent of the gross yearly profits so that she could take over all of the obligations of the business, and they negotiated the same deal with their fathers cousin Fred, who managed the clothing store, and both of them was grateful. The twins opened up a separate business accounts for them, so Kim and Fred could deposit the business funds into the bank, and the twenty percent of their profit would automatically be transferred into their bank accounts and the twins wouldn't have to handle any of the money part of the business dealings at all. The twins had Attorney Parker draw up a contract and the deal was signed.

The twins went and rented a nice apartment in Durango Colorado just in case they had to make a quick get away. They took the furniture out of the stash spot, and took it to the new apartment along with some guns, 150 g's and the five keys of cocaine that they had left over from their father stash. Everything was going according to plan, when one day, Keyona and Teyona was in the

Corvette coming from the beauty salon and Keyona realized that they was being followed.

"Keyona said, Tey, Tey, we got a tail..!"

"Are you sure?" Teyona asked.

"Yeah, see that black Dodge Ram truck back there."

"Yeah."

"It's been following us every since we left the beauty salon."

"Can you see who it is?" Teyona said as she held her Gloc 9mm in her hand.

"No not yet, but get ready! When I turn this corner, I'm going to stop so you can get him!"

"O'kay." Teyona said as she unhooked her seat belt. Keyona then turned down a side street and stopped in the middle of the street as Teyona took aim over her seat. The convertible top was already down, so she had a clear view over the back of the Vett.

The black Dodge Ram truck turned the corner and stopped, as he looked down the barrel of Teyona's Gloc that she had pointed dead at him.

"Ain't this a bitch, it's Detective Jones!" Teyona said as Keyona punched out burning rubber down the street and Teyona started unloading her gloc into the Dodge Ram wind shield.

Detective Jones ducked just in the nick of time as the bullets penetrated his truck wind shield and the Corvette sped-off.

Detective Jones got out of his truck and looked at his wind shield that had nine bullet holes in it, six of the holes was where his head would have been. "Crazy Bitches, I knew it!" Detective Jones said to himself as he hit his hand on his hood. He knew that the twin's attorney put a restraining order on him, so he couldn't report it, because he might end up getting arrested for harassment. "I'll get you bitches, I promise you that!"

Keyona hit two corners and saw that the truck wasn't following them she looked over at her sister who was laughing out loud and Keyona said, "Tey, Tey why did you do that? That was the damn police, and he knows who we are!"

"Fuck him, we got a restraining order on his races ass, so who is he going to call and tell? He's under investigation, so he ain't considered a damn police no more. I hope that I killed his races ass!"

"Tey, Tey you're trippin now! If you shot him, then well be in jail by tomorrow."

"Come on Key, Key think about it...! He's a civilian now, and he wasn't suppose to be around us, so we had every right to defend ourselves, when we got a dangerous, crazy, and violent man after us. We can call the police and have him arrested if we wanted to."

"I hope that you're right, because if not, then that could have fucked up our plans." Keyona said as she shook her head and Teyona started busting up laughing.

"Listen Key, Key, trust me!"

"I'm not saying that I don't trust you, but we just got to be smarter we could've talked to him instead of shooting at him."

"Fuck that…! He got what he asked for, now go by the reservoir so I can throw this Gloc in the creek.." Teyona said as she cut back up the music as Tupac song; 'My ambition of a rider' bumped through the woofers of the expensive sound system.

When they got home, Teyona called Red Rum and told him what had happened, just in case they got arrested for it, and go to jail. This way Red Rum would be able to finish off Big Al for them.

"So did you get him?" Red Rum asked.

"I'm not sure Unc!"

"You should've got out and finished his bitch ass off."

"I know, but speed racer here punched out." And they laughed as Keyona rolled her eyes.

"Don't worry I got your back Angels…the family sends their love too!"

"Tell them that we said hi."

"O'kay Angel, holla back you hear!"

"We will…bye."

She hung up as she looked over at Keyona and said, your secret admire Itty Bitty said what's up!"

"That's your secret admire."

"He is kind of cute, I might have to give him some before he leaves." Teyona said with a nasty smile.

"You're going crazy girl… I better put some of this weed in a condom, so if the police come and get us tonight, I can put it up in my coochie, and then I'll at least be able to get high while I'm mad at you!"

"Fuck you girl…! Make me one too." Teyona said as they started bustin' up laughing.

* * * *

Red Rum and his crew was rolling around looking for the right move, as they drove around the streets in a new 88 Cutless G-ride, that they had Nina buy out of the car auto buy news paper. Nina was driving and Red Rum was sitting in the passenger seat as Itty Bitty said, "Did

Teyona say that the police was in a black Dodge Ram truck?"

"Yep." Red Rum said.

"Look...!" Itty Bitty pointed at the black Ram truck that had the front wind shield shot up.

"Well I guess that he didn't get shot yet...baby pull over there."

Red Rum said as they followed him in the Taco Bell parking lot.

Red Rum and Nina jumped out and he hugged her as they approached Detective Jones truck. Detective Jones got out of his truck and seen a big Chrome 357 Magnum and a Gloc 9mm pointed at him.

"If you do anything stupid, I'm gonna shoot the shit out of you."

"O'kay don't shoot me man, do you know who I am?"

"Do it look like I give a damn?" Red Rum said as he grabbed the gun from Detective Jones waste band. Then he found his handcuffs and said "put your damn hands behind you back!"

"What a minute." Detective Jones said as Red Rum slapped him up-side of his head with the barrel of the gun, and knocked him to the ground as he handcuffed him and found another gun strapped to his ankle. Then they drugged Detective Jones and threw him in the back seat of the Cutless as Itty Bitty pulled up. Red Rum jumped in the back seat with him, as Nina jumped in the front seat, and Itty Bitty drove off.

Teyona received a phone call from Red Rum and she looked over at Keyona and said, "Unc wants to meet us in the back of Jack In The Box in the alley. They grabbed their guns and got dress in jeans and big dark coats, and took the rent a car as they drove off.

The twins pulled up at the location and seen Red Rum and his crew standing by a green 88 Cutless, and the twins got out of the rent a car and walked over and said, "What's up uncle Red?"

"Oh we just having a little fun tonight and wanted to know if you wanted to join us?"

"What do you got in mind?" Keyona said curiously as every one was smiling.

Red Rum popped the trunk of the 88 Cutless and Detective Jones was laying in it, butt naked and hogged tied with his eye swollen.

"Oh shit, look it's the smart guy." Teyona said as she laughed. Keyona seen him and turned her head for a brief moment, then realize that it was to late, and turned back around as Teyona said, "who's the smart one now you races son-of-a-bitch, with your little dick ass....you ain't so tuff now huh – welcome to death row punk!"

"Do you want to do the honors?" Red Rum asked Teyona.

"Hell ya, I'll kill his sorry races ass." Teyona said as the Detective eyes watered as he seen death in Teyona's eyes and he knew that it was over for him. And also, to make matter worse, realize that his hunch was right.

"Give me a knife somebody!" Teyona said.

"Here baby, you can use mine." Itty Bitty said as he smiled at Teyona gangsta ways. She was surely his type, but he still wanted them both!

Teyona grabbed the knife and said I'll see you in hell you races son – of –a- bitch," and she cut off his dick, as he squalled with the duck tape over his mouth. Red Rum and Itty Bitty grabbed their dicks and said....Ooowow!"

"You won't need that! Not like it was worth anything." And her and Nina started laughing.

"Just kill him and get it over with Tey, Tey!" Keyona said with authority as Teyona looked at her, and looked back at the Detective and said, "You're lucky!" And she stabbed the knife right through his heart and watched him shiver, and shake as he shitted on himself, and die instantly.

"Yeah, ya'll are related – it's no question about that! Itty Bitty said.

Red Rum pulled out the knife and wiped it off on the Detective's hair, and said, "Ya'll follow us, so we can get rid of this piece of shit, and then ya'll can drop us back off at the apartment."

The twins jumped in their rent a car with Itty Bitty as Nina and Red Rum took the body over in Crip hood, and set the car on fire with the body in the trunk. They ran and jumped in the rent a car as they went over to Red Rum and his crew's little apartment and kicked it for the rest of the night. The girls asked questions about their father, and heard stories that they enjoyed and would remember for the rest of their life. Every one passed out and Teyona gave Itty Bitty some pussy to show her appreciation for his devotion and sacrifice. And he made sure that he enjoyed every bit of the fantasy as Teyona said, "I don't know why they call your ass Itty Bitty, because that name don't even fit you at all."

He blushed as they fell asleep cuddled in each other arms.

Chapter 13
The Double Cross

The next day Detective Jones murder was all over the news. Big Al was mad as hell when he seen it, because he knew that because the Detective body was found in his hood, meant that his money would be fucked up, because the dope street was on fire now and swarming with cops. The police was snatching up every nigga from the hood that they could catch. So the little homeboys had to set up shop at certain smoker's houses, so they could try to maintain their hustle.

Big Al put out the word for all of his workers to try to lay low, until the block cool off a bit. He was over at his new stash spot with Gwen laying low, and having her cater to his wound. Gwen played like she was on her period, so Big Al didn't want no pussy, he just made her suck him off when he woke up, and enjoyed her bom head game.

Jim Jim paged Big Al, and said that they were out of work and the workers were setting up spots at local base head houses, and is in need of some more dope. Big Al told him to meet him at his sister's house on Elm St. in an half hour. Then he looked over at Gwen and said, "Get your ass up and get dress! I need you to drive me to a couple of places today, so I can handle some business, then after I'm through, you can go do what you want to do. You hear me?"

Gwen shook her head, "yes," but at the same time, her emotion was growing enraged at the fact that Big Al just felt that he could talk to her and order her around just any oh way. He had no respect for her, and she wondered how she ever allowed herself to tolerate his sorry ass this long.

Gwen shook her thoughts off, as she got up and went into the bathroom to get dress.

Big Al went into the closet and grabbed his last five kilo's of cocaine, and knew that he would have to re-cope soon, and hoped that the police would ease up off his young homeboys soon, so he could get his business flowing right. "Damn." He cursed as he thought about the dumb ass nigga who killed that policemen and put him in the hood. He knew that he had a lot of young wild homeboy's who didn't give a damn about killin, but why in the fuck couldn't they think more. He thought to himself as he put the dope in a duffle bag and got dressed.

* * * *

Little Willie went into Baby Insane's apartment building to deliver to him the four ounces that Baby Insane ordered. He served him then left and when Little Willie got back to his undercover bucket, which was a 75 Nova, he saw that the back tire was flat. "Damn!" He said as he kicked the flat tire and went over to the trunk to grab the spare tire and jack. As he was moving stuff around trying to get to the spare tire, a voice said, "Check mate bitch." And before Little Willie could react, a 44 bulldog blow the whole top of his dome off.

The masked man ran around the block and jumped in a g-ride and drove off, as he took off his mask and CK said, "Domu that one was for you my nigga."

Baby Insane ran out side of his apartment with his gloc 9mm clinched in his hand, as he seen Little Willie layed out in the trunk of his Nova with his dome blown off. Baby Insane said, "Shit..!" And looked around and went into Little Willie's pocket and grabbed all of his money, his jewelry and his 45 automatic, then ran to the back of the apartment building and counted his come up. He got the 44 hundred dollars that he just gave Little Willie for the ounces, and an extra 7 g's and about 15 g's worth of jewelry. A smoker named Bill walked up and

180

said; "Now that was fucked up! Ain't that your homeboy you just robbed like that? That's crazy! Listen here, give me a half ounce and I'll go and get rid of the body for you. I know that you don't want that kind of heat in front of your spot!"

"You're right, go get rid of it for me, and when you come back I'll have that for you, but meet me at the liquor store!"

"You got it." Bill said as he ran out front to where Little Willie was and throw Little Willie in the trunk of the Nova and reached into his pocket and grabbed his car keys as he jumped in the Nova and drove it ten blocks on the flat tire, then searched it and found a big 357 magnum under the seat and a small leather bag with 5 g's in it. Bill said, "Jack pot," then he wiped the car down and locked it, then left.

He made it to where Baby Insane told him to meet him at, and as Bill arrived Baby Insane looked real paranoid as he escorted Bill toward the back of the liquor store, but he was looking around like he was up to something. Bill nonchalantly reached one hand into his old coat pocket, and grabbed the butt of the big 357 magnum as they were walking, and once they got to the back alley-way behind the store, Baby Insane said, "you should have minded your own business cuzz," and reached for his 45 automatic that he had in the back of his belt. Bill shot twice through his old coat and knocked Baby Insane into the bushes.

Bill said, "No Cuzz, you should've known who you was fuckin with, I started this gangsta shit punk." Then he shot Baby Insane one more time in the heart and said, "I'm triple OG Big Crip, nigga!" Bill aka Big Crip from Rollin 30's reached down and took Baby Insane's guns, money, drugs, and the jewelry that he had on, which he stole from Little Willie. Then he ducked down into the alley as he disappeared through the short cuts.

* * * *

Big Al pulled up at his sister's house on Elm street, and Jim Jim was waiting. Gwen pulled up and seen Jim Jim and her pussy instantly got wet. Jim Jim walked up to Gwen's Escalade truck as Big Al was getting out, and Jim Jim said, What's up Loc!"

"Man, too much shit!" Big Al uttered as he got out of the truck slow and limped, because his butt was aching.

"It must be a real pain in the ass!" Jim Jim joked as everyone laughed and Big Al said, "Oh, you got jokes huh!"

"I'm just playing cuzz, good to see that you got nine lives."

"Yeah, them bitch ass nigga's tried to catch the triple OG slippin, but you know, I buss my heat like a cowboy!"

"That's right Loc! What's up Ms Gwen! I see that you got your ride and die bitch with you." And they laughed as Gwen blushed.

"Yeah, she's a rider." Big Al admitted. Then Big Al looked at the book bag that Jim Jim had and said, "How much money is that?"

"This is 108 g's – Little Willie got the rest for you.

"Cool, that's 5 keys there. Ya'll be extra careful, because the block is hot, the pigs is snatching nigga's up like slaves, about that murder that happened to that punk ass police that was found in the trunk of that burning car in the hood.

"Yeah, I heard! Nigga's must've stepped there game up." Jim Jim said with a smile.

"Yeah that's cool, but don't shit were you got to eat at."

"You're right about that, because that really fuck business up! Maybe them Bloods put that down, and just left us holding the blame."

"Possibly, maybe we should set up shop in one of their neighborhoods, you know, on the boarder line or something!"

"That might be a good option, but we need to get rid of that nigga CK so they won't have no direction, and we can just have our way with them. Especially considering that, Domu and Sin ain't around no more." And they both started smiling.

"Good idea, tell the homeboys that I got a 25 thousand dollar reward for whoever drops CK."

"You got that Big Al, let me go and handle this business and I'll get with you later."

"Cool and be careful cuzz!"

"You too!" Jim Jim said as they gave one another their secret hand shake and departed.

Big Al jumped back in the truck and said, "Take me to my main house so I can get my Bentley."

Gwen looked at him and smiled, as she drove him to his main house. She only been there once at night, and forgot how to get there, so this would be a real pleasure.

Big Al gave Gwen the directions and when they arrived at the front gates to Big Al's seven bedrooms plushed out mini mansion, Big Al grabbed the book bag out of the back seat and said, "I'll come and pick up the other money from the condo later." Then he got out of the Escalade truck and limped into his plushed out dwellings.

Gwen rolled her eyes as she got pissed that Big Al didn't invite her in. Every since she told him that she was on her period he's been acting funny like she was contaminated or something. "Fuck that short funny style nigga!" Gwen thought to herself as she drove away.

When people seen Big Al for the first time, they were taken back by his appearance, because he only stand 5' 6'' and possess a cubby thick built. But, because of his light skin, everyone considered him a pretty boy type, with hazel eyes, and long wavy hair, that he wear in a ponytail or long braids. He caught his first body in high school and got out of juvenile hall at the age of 21, and began his enterprise, after robbing and killing the Mexican brothers, who had his neighborhood on lock when he came home from juvenile. Big Al robbed them for over 300 g's and 15 kilo's, and it was on and poppin every since. He gave his little homeboys jobs, and everyone's been eating good every since, so they admired and looked up to him, as another gangsta tail was born.

Gwen went to get her hair done at the hair solon that everyone like going to, "True Beauty." And as always it was packed. "Kim I got that twenty dollars for you."

Gwen said as she walked over to Kim's area. That was their special code so Kim would know that Gwen would give her an extra twenty dollars if Kim would slip her into an early appointment. Kim just had a girl cancel on her, so she said, "you're right on time! I thought that you was going to miss your appointment girl...! Robin!!! Come and wash Gwen's hair, and condition it for me!"

"O'kay Kim – come on Gwen! I'll get you hooked up." Robin said as Kim and Gwen smiled, and Gwen followed Robin toward the sink area.

Teyona was sitting in Kim's chairs getting her hair done, as she looked up at Kim and said "you think that you got all that game."

"You know that a sista got to have a little finesse about herself," Kim said as they laughed. Teyona caught on to Kim's little secret code and laughed at how slick she did it.

Teyona and Keyona treated Nina to the beauty salon so Nina could get her lady thang on. Red Rum wanted Nina to get one of those sexy short Toni Braxton hair cuts, to change her appearance and to compliment her beautiful facial feature. Nina was more then happy to comply with his desires.

* * * *

Captain Davis was in his office with Detective Smith and Detective Marshall who's the Lieutenant over the drug enforcement department. The Captain just received an ugly call from the Governor of Denver Colorado, and he gave the Captain the green light to intervene into the gang war, that was polluting the streets of Denver. Detective Jones murder was just to much to handle, and it was time to even the score.

"I want every one of those fucking gang bangers in the prisons by next week, and if they resist, then use any force needed to deal with it. I want every one of these young crazy black gangster thugs, out of my damn city before the week is up. We got the Fed's talking about coming to take over our town, and you know what that means...! 'Marshal Law!' Now do what you got to do and do it quick..!"

"Yes Sir." The two detectives said as they stood up and walked out of the Captain's office.

Detective Smith looked at Detective Marshall and said, "have your task force team briefed and in full riot gear tomorrow morning at 7a.m., it's time to sweep these damn streets, and I mean by any means necessary!"

"We'll be ready." Detective Marshall said as he smiled and rubbed his hands together and walked to his office to tell his team the good news.

* * * *

Red Rum was picking up Nina from the beauty salon as Gwen walked out from getting her hair whipped she recognized him and then Nina, and she knew that she seen her somewhere when she glanced at her in the Beauty Salon, but didn't recognize her because the change in her appearance with her new short hair cut. Gwen ducked on the side of her truck, and then smiled and walked over to Red Rum black Tahoe. When Itty Bitty seen her approaching, he instantly pulled out his 45 automatic and pointed it at her. Red Rum seen Itty Bitty reaction, and looked to his side as he saw Gwen hold her hands up where he could see them, and he held up his hand to tell Itty Bitty to hold up.

"Hey dark and handsome! Please don't hurt me, I'm coming with respect." Gwen said.

"What's up little momma, what do you got on your mind?" Red Rum said as Nina walked up on side of Gwen with her hand inside of her big Fend; purse.

"Listen, you showed me a lot of love a while back, and I wanted to repay you for your realness!"

"How so little momma?"

"I know where Big Al's main house is!"

Red Rum's eyes deemed as he said, "give her your purse, and jump in the back of the truck."

"You promise that you won't kill me if I give you the information?"

"As long as you're not trying to cross us, or deceive us. Then you're cool."

"I'm not! I'm straight up with you. You know that my word is all that I got, and I stand on it!"

"O'kay little momma, you got my word!" Red Rum said as Gwen gave Nina her purse, and walked and jumped in the back seat of the truck with Itty Bitty.

Itty Bitty said, "What's up sexy, how's my favorite gangsta bitch doing?"

"I'm trying to survive and move on with my life, that's all."

"You can do it!" Itty Bitty said as he put his 45 automatic on his lap, and held it gently in a self protecting way.

"So what's on your mind little mamma?" Red Rum asked.

"Listen man, I'm going to keep it one hundred percent with you, and you can accept it any way you want." Red Rum shook his head as Gwen said, "I'm in love with one of Big Al's workers, and we are about to take Big Al's stash and leave town! However, I know that once Big Al finds out what we've done, then he's going to be a big threat to us for life, and I don't need that, because if he ever do catch up to us, then he'll kill us for sure. At one time I thought that he cared for me, and respected me, but later on I realized that he was just using me and will possibly kill me if he get's tired of me. I was thinking about killing his bitch ass myself, but I don't want to harbor a cold hearted murder on my conscious like that, because he never really gave me a justified reason for me to go there. Yeah, he treats me like shit sometimes, but that's just because I allowed my self to tolerate it. Anyway, like I said, me and my man is out of here real soon. So you wanna know where the nigga lives at, then I'll tell you, and the rest is on you! Just make sure that he doesn't live to get revenge on me and my man. That's all that I asked?"

"I feel you little momma, and I respect your feelings. His time is already limited, and I can assure you that he will never be able to hurt you again! Take your man and go live happy ever-after together. You got my blessings.

"Thank you, do you have a pen and a piece of paper?" Gwen asked as Nina gave her one, and she wrote down Big Al's address and handed it to Red Rum.

"Good looking out baby! Take care of yourself o'kay!"

"I will…!" Gwen said as she got out of the truck and smiled at Itty Bitty and Nina. Nina took Gwen's 3.80 automatic out of Gwen's purse and dropped the clip out and ejected the bullets that was in the chambers and put it back in her purse, then she handed the purse back to Gwen.

"Got to always be cautious!" Nina said as Gwen just giggled and shook her head and left.

* * * *

Jim Jim was hustling all day, dropping off and picking up dope. His phone rang as he walked into the new stash spot.

"Hello!"

"Hi baby." Gwen said in her sexy voice.

"What's up princess…I was just thinking about you!" Jim Jim said.

"I was thinking of us too baby. I'm ready to leave, let's just pack up our shit and leave tonight. We got enough money to go any where and live a good life. You can take all of the dope that you got from him today, and I can grab all the money that I got of his, plus… everything that I got save up, would be like 200 g's..! Come on baby, let's just leave and go start a new! Me and you, the world is ours."

"You know what Princess, your absolutely right! Go pack all of you shit, and meet me at the Travel Lodge Motel in an hour, and we're out of this State tonight!"

"O'kay baby, thank you! I love you baby…. You make me so happy. I'll be there in an hour o'kay, bye!"

"Bye, bye!" Gwen said as she hung up her cell phone, and prayed that Big Al didn't catch them before they left or show up at the Condo as she's gathering her stuff up, because if he did, then she knew that she would have to kill him herself, because Gwen would never let Big Al mess up her future dreams.

* * * *

Teyona saw Gwen enter into Red Rum's Tahoe truck, and then leave out smiling and waving, as she jumped into her Escalade truck and left.

Teyona put Keyona up on what just took place and they both walked out to Red Rum truck after Gwen drove away, and Teyona said, "What was that all about Unc?"

"That there is our wish come true! That's Big Al's bitch, the one that I told you was at the stash spot with that Paper incident." Anyway...apparently, Big Al has been dogging her out, and her and one of Big Al's workers is in love, and about to take Big Al's stash and run away with it. She don't want her past to catch up with her, so she gave us his address to his main house. Now, it's time to put an end to this shit!"

"Good", Keyona said. "We're going to go get dress and meet ya'll at your apartment."

"We'll be waiting young tender." Red Rum said as they departed and went to go get ready.

* * * *

Big Al was over to Tina's new townhouse enjoying a 'ménage a trios' with her and her girl friend name Abby a.k.a. Taboo! Taboo was a pretty blonde hair white girl that was thick in all of the right places, and a fat round butt like a sista. Taboo and Tina worked together at PT's the local strip club that's real popular with the ballers. Tina and Taboo had a relationship going on real open with one another, and they both enjoyed a little dick every now and then, and Big Al is usually the only male participant.

Big Al was exhausted as he made it to Gwen's new condo at 12:40a.m. and thought about making Gwen suck the left over juices from his nuts, before he jump in the shower, and then he laughed to himself as he opened up the door and walked in. Everything looked o'kay as he clinched his big 44 desert eagle in his hand, using precaution as he entered his residence, like he always did. He limped his way up stairs, and when he got to the bedroom he looked around, and Gwen wasn't in the bed sleep like she usually is. "Where's that bitch this late at night?" He said to himself, and then walked passed the closet and saw Gwen's clothes missing. He limped into the closet and saw that the safe was open and all of his money was gone. "Ain't this a bitch! I can't believe that this hoe got the heart to try to play me like this, I'll kill her if I catch her scandalous ass!" Big Al said out loud to himself as he called up Little Willie and didn't get an answer, so he called up Jim Jim, and nobody answered his phone either. So Big Al limped back down to his car and jumped in it and drove back to his new stash spot. He limped up and stairs and went in, and he witnessed one of the worse feelings in the world... 'Betrayal.' All of the dope was gone and Big Al was enraged with anger. "I'll kill all of them dirty son of a bitches! They got me fucked up." Big Al tried to call Jim Jim and Little Willie one more time and wondered which one of them was it that betrayed him… or was it both of them, or maybe all of them. He went back down to his car and went on the hunt for them all.

He went over to Jim Jim's condo and creep around to see if he seen Jim Jim's new Chrysler 300, and it wasn't in it's parking stall. So Big Al went around and knock on the door, but when no one came to answer, he kicked the door in, and ran up-stairs with his gun drawn and notice that all of Jim Jim's clothes and personal stuff was gone. "Dirty Muthafucka!" Big Al said, as he laughed and then search around for some sort of clue or evidence. When he couldn't find none, he thought about Little Willie and limped back to his car, so he could go see if he was at home.

Big Al got to Little Willie's apartment and saw his Mustang parked out back in his parking stall, so he went and knock on Little Willie's apartment door, and when nobody came to answer it, big Al kicked it in and ran in with his gun drawn and ready to shoot. He saw that Little Willie wasn't home, so he search and saw that none of

Little Willie's stuff was missing. So he tried to call him again, but no answer. He found Little Willie's stash and counted 20 g's and put it in his pocket as he left out and drove around looking for all of his betrayers. He stopped at his sister's house on Elm Street, and gave her the 20 g's to hold for him. He put on some black jeans, black leather Nike's, and a black sweat shirt with a hood, and a black leather jacket, then he grabbed his AR 15 and two extra hundred round clips, and the extra clip to his 44 Desert Eagle, and gave his sister the keys to his Bentley G.T. in exchange for her new Lexus, and then he went on a mission looking for his enemies, and his so called best friend and associates!

Chapter 14
I Ride For My Niggas

Big Al was on the dope street posted up in Ms. Ford yard as he told Tic and Creep how Jim Jim and Gwen played him. He put out a $100 thousand dollar bounty on their heads, and knew that a nigga would sell his own mother out for that kind of money. Big Al was smoking some weed and sippin some Hennessy, as him, Tic and creep talked about re-establishing their enterprise and overcoming their losses. Big Al liked both of them, because they where young, smart, and down, and the way that they stuck together he knew that they had a sense of loyalty about themselves. It was 8:30 on a Saturday morning, and the block was clocking in full swing. All the little homeboys was standing out in the cut, and behind cars slanging rocks, and the crack head was either running up to their favorite dope dealer begging for as much dope as their money can buy.

Crip, Chip, Scrappy and G-Pain all was in Uncle Rambo house, pulling a train on two young white smoked out girls, who just got turned out on the pipe and ran out of money while they were sprung dumb, so as always, collateral was the next best thing, and their bodies became their negotiation tool. Uncle Rambo was a triple OG homeboy who went to the Army and got caught up in Desert Storm, and came back missing a leg, and mentally insane. He started smoking rock as his crunch for his pain and insanity, and smoked up his VA disability and Social Security checks faster then he could get them. He had mad love for his young homeboys who he refer to as his young solders, and he always let them rent his guess bedrooms out for their little freaknic's as long as they hook him up with some rocks, then they can trick all they want. Uncle Rambo always ended up with all of the young hoe's that they turned out anyway, so he felt that he was in a win, win, situation.

Big Al was sitting in his sister car that was parked in Ms. Ford driveway, and rappin with his two new lieutenants when a gang of undercover police cars started pulling up every where.

"What the fuck!" Big Al said as Tic and Creep ducked down and watched all the police task force jump out and start chasing all the homeboys. Robert Jr ran and tried to jump over a brick fence in front of Mr. Ed's house, so he could make his get away, but a task force officer unloaded a 12 gauge riot pump at his back, hitting him and splattering him all over the brick wall.

"Cuzz they killed Robert Jr., they shot him in cold blood! Get them muthafucka's cuzz." Big Al ordered as he grabbed his AR-15 from his side, and came up bussin like a true gangsta. Tic and Creep saw his reaction and pull their guns out and started firing at the police too, and all the homeboys stop running when they saw Big Al and them getting off, and turned around and started shooting at the police too.

Big Al's AR-15 ripped through the police that shot Robert Jr., and layed him twisted in the hot streets. Then he hit two more police who was 20 feet a head of him as they turned to late to see it coming. Tic shot at police who had Lady C on the ground, and fell down holding his side from the impact. Lady C then grabbed the police 45 automatic from it's hoster, and shot the police in the face five times, and as she jumped up an officer sprayed her with a round from his AR-15 police addition and dropped her dead.

Then the police started shooting at Big Al, Tic, and Creep as they hid behind Big Al's sister Lexus. The police didn't expect a shoot out like this and Detective Marshall called for back up as he was ducking behind a car exchanging shots with Crips as they came out of the wood work.

Crip-crip, Chip, and C-Pain was fucking the two girls when they heard the gun fire, and Scrappy ran into the bedroom and said, "hey cuzz, the homeboys is having a shoot out with the pigs... Come on!" Crip-crip, Chip, and C-Pain jumped up and put on their pants and shoes, and grabbed their guns and ran out side to help their homeboys. They all ran out of the front door, and ducked behind the trees and concrete walls in uncle Rambo front yard, and saw that they were in back of two of the police car where Seven police was ducking behind exchanging gun fire.

Scrappy said, "let's ride cuzz," and they smiled and jumped up bussin. They caught the police by surprise and dropped four, and wounded two out of the seven, as the two wounded police and the other one started shooting back at them, and Crip-Crip got caught slippin as a task force police jumped and rolled from behind a park car and shot Crip-crip in the chest three times with an 357 magnum, then jumped behind a big tree and started exchanging shits with Scrappy and C-Pain. "He got Crip-crip cuzz, Kill that cracker!" C-pain said as he jumped up bussin his 45 automatic fearlessly, as his 45 clicked and ran out of bullets on him. The task force officer seen his chance, so he ran up shooting at Scrappy with his 9mm

Gloc and took a good aim at C-Pain, as he was hiding behind the tree with no ammo, and C-Pain tried his best to cover up his face and head when he saw the task force police running up aiming their big 357 magnum at him, and shot the two bullets into C-Pain head, killing his instantly.

Scrappy got off a shot at the task force police, but only hit him in the chest where the bullet proof vest stopped it. The task force office stopped and rolled behind the house and reloaded his gun.

Big Al and his lieutenant's was almost out of bullets as they seen four more police cars pull up and sixteen more police jumped out and took cover as they started picking off the gang members who was hiding behind trees, cars, and houses. "Shit!" Big Al mumbled as he jumped back up and unloaded his AR-15 into the closes police car to him, dropping two officers as a gang of bullets came back at him and just missed him as he ducked behind his sister Lexus, and the bullets ate the body to the car up.

Uncle Rambo busted out the attic window to his house, and shot what looked like a rocket launcher from his window and blow-up the second police car killing six officers as they layed dead around the burning police vehicle. Uncle Rambo had a M-16 rifle with an M-203 rocket launcher attachment to it, that he got as a present from his Captain in the Army for saving his life. The Captain was an arms dealer and had a connection with the black market. Uncle Rambo unloaded a hundred round clip into the police caravan, and diverted all their attention to him. He hollered "Armageddon!!!" and reloaded the rocket launcher and put another clip in, as he shot another police vehicle, blowing it up.

Big Al looked over and seen Tic and Creep layed out on the grass twisted, and he took off toward the back of Ms. Fords yard, and hopped her back fence into the other neighbors back yard, and started hitting yards and fences through short cuts that lead further and further away from the shoot out. As he was running he saw an old white man getting into his new Nisan 300ZX and Big Al pulled out his big Desert Eagle 44 on him and said, "I need to borrow your car!"

"Take it..!" the old man said as he gave Big Al the keys and watch him jump in his car and punch out.

Big Al saw that the police had the dope street blocked off, so he laughed and turned off in the other direction as he headed for his baby mansion in Cherry Creek.

Scrappy saw Uncle Rambo putting it down, so he tried to run back into Uncle Rambo's house, but got gunned down by the task force office who was on the side of the house. Then the task force officer creped through Uncle Rambo's front door, and he saw two young white girls half naked in the far end corner of the house hugged up. He was pissed at the sight, knowing that the black thugs had to have kidnapped them and rapping the two girls.

The task force officer eased up the stairs as he seen Uncle Rambo unloading another clip at the police officers outside, and laughing at the same time. Uncle Rambo went to reload his gun, and saw out of the corner of his eyes a figure creeping up stairs, so he went for his 45 automatic in his belt and pulled it out, but at the same time he felt the bullets from the task force officer gun enter into his body. Fortunately, all the cocaine in Uncle Rambo's system had him pumped-up so much that he was unable to feel the vicious rounds of bullets that ripped through his body, so that he was able to get off three more shots before he fell from the second story window. The cops, who were outside the house, ran up and shot Uncle Rambo 50 more times, and he died with an ugly smile on his face. When Uncle Rambo got off his shots, two of the bullets hit Detective Marshall special task force officer in the shoulder and vest. The one that hit him in the bullet proof vest was right in the heart area, so the vest save him from his soul being escorted through the fire of hell's gates.

After Uncle Rambo died the shooting came to a bloody end. Those who didn't die in the shoot out or run when they had a chance, was arrested and charged with murder, attempted murder, drug charges, or the new terrorist act, which basically states that, 'If you're in a gang or drug enterprise, and one of your members get caught doing a criminal act, then you can also get charge with the same offense, even though you never participated in the act or had any knowledge of the crime. The law was bias, and the street niggas' was its main target, and today many was about to feel its raft.

Chapter 15
Murder Mafia For Life

At the same time that Detective Marshall was raiding the Crips dope street, Detective Smith was leading a raid on the Crenshaw Mafia's dope block. All of the homies was standing out hustling as the police caravan hit the block. A neighborhood smoker seen them coming and hollered "5-O... 5-O!" And all of the homies started running and throwing away guns and dope, as the Task Force jumped out and gave chase. The task force officers started drawing down on nigga's who didn't run, or thought that they were safe because they were standing in their own front yard, and to their surprise, the task force officers grabbed them up too. The majority of the nigga's got caught because the police was anticipating them running and had the block surrounded.

CK was laying in the bed with Suzzy when he heard all of the commotion outside. He jumped up and grabbed his twin gloc's and looked out of the window and seen police every where running around chasing his homies as they tried to make a quick get away.

"I'm glad you're in here with me," Suzzy said.

"I'm glad too snow bunny." He uttered as he watched the police handcuffed and detained his little homies. The police set them all on the curve next to each other, women and children too. After that the police kicked in two smoker's houses that were known to be the main dope spots in the hood. Luckily, no shots were fired and the raid went smoothly. All in all the task force arrested 24 people. Fourteen of them were known Bloods and drug dealers, and ten of them were just smokers that got caught up in the mix of things.

The police gave each other a high five as they went around and found guns and drug's that nigga's throw as they tried to run. The police brought in K-9 units, and what the officers didn't find, the dogs found, and what the dogs didn't find, the base-heads who came after the police left, found.

* * * *

Red Rum, Nina, Itty Bitty and the twins was all sitting in a 89 Cadillac Fleetwood with tinted windows, staking out Big Al's baby mansion in Cherry Creek, that Gwen gave them the address to. They been there all night waiting for him to arrive, but he never showed. Keyona, Nina, and Itty Bitty just woke up from their slumber, and was pissed that Big Al didn't come home yet. Teyona and

Red Rum was talking all night as they stayed up waiting for Big Al to come home.

"What time is it Poppy?" Nina asked as she yawned and stretched.

"It's 9 a.m."

"Damn this nigga might never show up!" Teyona said.

"Fuck that, let's just wait him out for a little while longer. I'm tired of this shit, it's time to put an end to this chapter in our life, so we can go on with our future. Keyona firmly said.

"I feel you on that little momma, this city is on fire right now. It ain't a good place to be, no telling when one of these nigga's is going to run up on me, and try to lay me down. This war that we kicked off is major, and nigga's is not asking a nigga what set he's from before he buss! It's like every gang is for themselves. I've been watching the news and the number of casualties that happened since we kick it off is over 30 niggas that has gotten killed. At first it was only 3 or 4 niggas a month, so you can imagine what those crackers are thinking." Red Rum said.

"Man them crackers don't give a fuck about no niggas, they probably left a truck full of guns parked in the hood, to make sure that these niggas do it right. I wouldn't put it pass them to dress up as rival gang members, and go shot some niggas themselves. All they're going to do is let these niggas kill each other off and then, the ones who are left around after this war is over, is going to get gaffled up and put in prison for the rest of their lives." Itty Bitty expressed.

"Damn, you talk like you care about these nigga's or something." Teyona said as she stared at him confused with her pretty face half balled up.

"Listen T, I'm here because my main man family got done wrong by some sorry ass niggas...and his fight is my fight too, we're family – that means Murder Mafia for life! But I don't get at a nigga on no gang bangin shit, unless he got problems with me or my family. Just to kill a nigga because we don't understand each other ain't my style. I'm bigger then that... I chase money, not niggas! But I meet all problems and threats head on, cause I'm a gangsta by nature." Itty Bitty expressed his thoughts strongly as Teyona shook her head in agreement. Red Rum just smiled at his comrade thoroughness in representing and checking a bitch!

"We got movement!" Keyona said as she saw a Nisan 300ZX pull up to Big Al's front gate and a person keyed in a code on the electric gate panel, and the gates opened and the 300ZX pulled up into the driveway.

"That's him!" Teyona said excitingly.

"Wait!" Red Rum said, "let him make it in and get relaxed, and we'll creep up and catch him slippin. Here Teyona, I want you and Keyona to wear these masks, because if he see's you two, then he will automatically know that he's dead, and we might not get him to open up the safe. After we get the money, then we'll let you two have your way with him, and Red Rum started laughing.

Now wait until we get up here, and then put on your mask. O'kay!"

"O'kay Unc!"

They got out of the car and crept into Big Al's yard. Big Al ran into his house and ran right to his safe and opened it, as he started pulling stacks of money in his big suit case. "Hey Cocaine." He said to his big white red nose American Pit Bull as his dog wagged his tail playfully and Big Al rubbed him down. He started grabbing some clothes and packed up another suit case. Then thought, "Damn, I better take a quick shower and get this gun powder residue off me, just in case I get pulled over." So he ran and jumped in the shower, and tried to scrub the gun residue off.

Big Al got out of the shower and got dress as he heard his dog attacking someone down stairs. He heard a scream and two gun shots as he grabbed his big 44 Desert Eagle from the bedroom door, and he seen his white Pit Bull laying on the white marble floor in a puddle of blood dead, and a pretty short hair lady getting up from the floor holding her arm.

"What the fuck!" Big Al said as he had his gun pointed at her, and then seen a movement run across the floor and shot at him as he turned and shot at the figure at the same time, and they both got hit when the guns fired together.

Big Al's bullet hit Red Rum in the left shoulder knocking him down from the impact, and Red Rum's bullet hit Big Al in the right arm knocking Big Al's gun out of his hand and landed on the ground.

Big Al looked up and seen three people running up the stairs shooting as he jumped back into his bedroom and slammed the door. Itty Bitty and the twins run full speed up the stairs, then Itty Bitty ran and kicked the bedroom door open, and the twins was right behind him bussin into the bedroom as the door swung open. Big Al was in motion when the door flew opened, and he droved out of his two story window, and rolled off of the roof onto the ground.

Teyona ran and jumped out of the window right in back of Big Al, and lost her balance as she rolled of the roof to the ground. Keyona turned back around and ran back down the stairs and said, "He jumped out of the window," as she passed up Nina and Red Rum. Itty Bitty climbed on the roof to see where Teyona went, and when he looked down, Big Al was standing over Teyona with Teyona's gun in his hand when he reached down and pulled off her mask and said, "It's you!" And in that split second that he pulsed in shock, cost him his life as Keyona unloaded her gloc into his body, and Itty Bitty finished him off with his 45 automatic from the roof top. Teyona looked up at Big Al and watch his soul get torn from his body as the bullets showed no mercy on him. Then she look over at Keyona and then at Itty Bitty.

Itty Bitty said, "Are you alright down there T"

"Yeah, I'm good, get the money and let's roll."

Itty Bitty ran back through the bedroom window, and grabbed the suit case with the money in it, and ran down stairs to catch up with everyone.

Keyona walked over and grabbed Teyona's mask from Big Al's grip, and said, "Let's get the hell out of here!"

They walked out to the Cadillac as Red Rum was using Nina and Keyona as his crutch, and the blood ran down his arm from his bullet wound.

Everybody jumped into the Cadillac as the neighbors was glancing out of there doors and windows. Teyona jumped into the driver seat, and sped off as she hit all side streets until she reached a comfortable distance from the mansion, and then jumped on the freeway as Teyona said, "we got to get him to a hospital."

"No, we can't go to no hospital. Go to the apartment," Red Rum said.

"O'kay Uncle, Key, Key keep pressure on it!"

"I am, just drive cool so you won't get pulled over.... We cant' afford a high speed chase, or a shot out with the police right now."

"Ya'll calm down.... He'll be alright, just drive to the apartment." Itty Bitty said.

They made it to the apartment safely. Itty Bitty started given orders like the little enforcer that he was groomed to be, "Nina, I want you to stay here and apply constant pressure to the wound. Keyona, I want you and Teyona to follow me!"

He grabbed a can of gas and jumped back into the Cadillac and drove twelve blocks over, and told the twins to wait around the corner as he drove in an alley, and set the Cadillac on fire, then ran and jumped in the rent a car with the twins and said, "go to the hospital now."

"Damn we got to go back and get Uncle now?"

"Girl quit asking me all of these damn questions, and do what the fuck I tell you to do! Itty Bitty said with authority, as Keyona just turned back around and punched out toward the hospital.

The pulled up and Itty Bitty seen his mark right off. He jumped out of the car and walked up to this older black lady and said, "Excuse me Ms are you a doctor?"

"Yes Sir, I am!"

Please forgive me Maam, I'm in dying need of your help. And he showed her his gun and said, "I'm not going to hurt you Maam, but my wife needs to see you, so can you please grab your medical bag and come with me."

She grabbed her bag and said, "I'll go, but please don't hurt me! I got a husband and three kids and they need me."

"I won't hurt you! I promise, just please come and help me." Itty Bitty grabbed her by the arm and walked her to the car and put her in the back seat and he slip in the back seat with her. Keyona looked at Teyona and drove off.

Teyona looked back and said, "Hi Maam, thank you so much for helping us.

"I don't think that I really had a choice Ms!" the female doctor gave a small laugh and glanced over at Itty Bitty.

"We won't hurt you Maam, we just need your experience and expertise and we'll bring you right back.

"O'kay, I'll do my best." The female doctor said.

Five minutes later, they walked the female doctor into the apartment, and the doctor saw Red Rum laying on the rug bleeding, as Nina was holding a towel over his wound with tears in her eyes. The doctor walked over and looked at the wound and said, "Good, you've stopped the bleeding already which means that no arteries were hit! You must've made some one real mad at you." Red Rum smiled as the female doctor reached into her medical bag and grabbed her long nose tweezers and long razor, then said, "Go boil me some water and I need that Hennessy, and you go grab me some more towels." The doctor

ordered and the girls complied. "Ya'll come over here so
you can learn how to do this, so you won't have to be
kidnapping people when you get yourself into this type of
predicament. Put that rag in his mouth, and let his gold
teeth bite down on it. You want to cut a small incision so
you can get to the bullet, give me that pencil. The doctor
poured some Hennessey on it, and then the doctor stuck it
into the wound and it went 3 1/2 inches into his shoulder.
"That's not too bad!" She grabbed the tweezers and stuck
it deep off into the wound, and fished the bullet out. Red
Rum was biting down on the towel, and letting out a
muffled holla sound. "You quit acting like a big baby, quit
playing the game, if you can't stand the pain!"

Everyone laughed as the doctor pulled out the big
slug. "Oh, that's a pretty big one," the doctor said, "Ya'll
hold him down tight, cause this is going to really test your
gangsta!"

Everyone tried to hide their laughter as the doctor
poured the Hennessy into his wound. Red Rum bit down
and screamed a painful sound, as a tear squeezed from the
corner of his eyes. "That's it, take it like a man! That's
called cowboy style!" And everyone laughed as the doctor
took out a sowing needle and medical thread from her bag

and started stitching up the wound, and then looked at Nina and said "Here baby, you finish him!"

"Oh, no you go ahead."

"Girl don't be no baby, you're in love with a gangsta, so you might as well learn now, so you'll know how to do it in the future. Now come here I'll teach you!" The doctor showed her what to do, and Nina finished stitching up the wound. "Now you need some rest, and eat something, cause that alcohol ain't going to help you regain your strength back."

"But it eases the pain." Red Rum muttered as he got up and kissed the doctor on the cheek and said, "You're an angle."

"So that mean's that you're not going to shot me, right!"

"Of course not baby, but I would like to ask you if you would please keep this little situation a secret from the authorities."

"You got my word Sir."

"Good." Red Rum said as she told Nina to clean up the doctors equipment and the blood! Then he grabbed four big bundles of money, and handed it to the doctor and said, "I really appreciate you baby."

"I appreciate you too Sir, and thank you so much!"

"You're welcome doc! Will ya'll drop her back off for me, and then come right back so we can talk."

"O'kay." Keyona and Teyona said as they walked the doctor out, and took her back to her car. They hugged, and then departed and the twins went back to the apartment.

When they arrived back at the apartment Red Rum, Nina and Itty Bitty had their stuff already packed into the truck. The apartment was cleaned up, and even the blood stain was scrubbed out of the rug. "We got to get out of here little momma. I like the old lady, but not enough to trust her with my freedom, you feel me?" Do you have somewhere we can lay low until tomorrow?" Red Rum asked as the girls shook their head yes!

"Come on follow us, you can come over to our stash house and kick it there." And they followed the twins to the stash spot where they could relax and count their come up.

* * * *

They all sat around the fire place and counted all the money that they took from Big Al's house. When they finished they had counted $1,650.000 dollars.

"O'kay, young tenders that's 300 g's that both of ya'll get!"

"Boy please, that's for ya'll. We're cool..!

"What, ya'll don't like money, ya'll really my type now!" Itty Bitty said as they started bustin' up.

"Oh, don't get it twisted, we love money! But, we're already rich, so we want ya'll to keep that, and understand that we really appreciate the way that ya'll came to our aid, when we needed that gangsta love, strength, and support, and know if you ever should need our support, then we are there for you in everyway."

"O'kay Double Trouble! I like that but listen, I've been hunted by this fantasy of making love to twins. You know, so how about making my fantasy a reality. It would be our little secret! Itty Bitty said as he licked his lips.

Teyona looked at Keyona and Keyona said, "Do you think that you can handle us both?"

"I'll die trying."

Everyone started laughing as Keyona said, "we might be able to accommodate you with that – you got rubbers?"

"I never leave home without them!" And he started smiling as he reached into his wallet and pulled out three new magnums.

"It takes a lot to fill up a magnum."

"I know! That's why I carry them." And he began smiling at them.

Chapter 16
Checkers Or Chest?

The next morning every body woke up feeling
revived. Red Rum, Itty Bitty, and Nina was glad that it
was finally over, and even more happy that they came up
on a couple of millions during the process. Now they can
go and enjoy their spoils of war. The twins was glad that it
was also over with because, now their father and Lala
could rest in peace and they can go enjoy the pleasure that
life offers with more contentment. The world was big and
full of interesting and exciting things to do, and they were
anxious to enjoy them all.

They all embraced and went their separate ways. A
new bound was created through blood and loyalty, and
the respect and devotion was unconditional. The twins
gather their little clothes that they wanted to take with
them, and put them in the trunk of the Vett, then went to
dropped the rent a car off, and then went to buy ten dozen
of red roses and went to put five on both their father's and
Lala's grave. They lite two candles by their grave site, and
said a few words to release their hidden thoughts and
emotions. They was at the foot of their father's and Lala's
grave as someone walked up and placed a single white
rose on both their father and Lala's grave. The twins

219

looked up and were startled by the present of Detective Smith from homicide division. He was in plan clothes but it was obvious that his gun was on his side.

"Hello Ladies!" I hope that I didn't startle you. Teyona looked over at her purse that was around 8 feet away from her. The Detective read her mind and said, "No need for that Ms. Fox, I come in peace! I just wanted to say good bye to you ladies before you leave, and extend my gratitude! We've been trying to stop and catch Big Al and his enterprise as well as Mr. Domu and Mr. Sin for the longest. But they we're way to slick and clever, and their crew members wouldn't snitch them out, so our hands was tide. They were some of the most vicious killer to ever come to this state, and we suspected them and their gang members for numerous murders around town. But no witnesses, and no evidence, meant no crime!

However, right after your father's and step mother's death, it seems like the murder rate between the Bloods and the Crips sky rocketed. That was the best thing that could have ever happen for this town, because them gang members didn't ever mean anybody any good. They robbed, stole, murdered, and sold dope to everyone with no respect for life. I was tempted to try to start a war between them all, to get rid of as many of them sick son of a bitches as possible. But even I must force myself to play by the rules, even though they didn't! Anyway, their war was a blessing to our war on crime, because as long as they was stupid enough to kill each other, then all we had to do is keep count of the bodies, and that was the fun part. 'The predator became the prey!' The higher ups even gave us orders to not intervene, and to let them kill each other off. Because as long as they were busy killing each other, then they were helping us out tremendously on our war on crime. In two weeks, I got 45 dead gang members laying in the morgue. Ten of them were from the shoot out that occurred yesterday on Federal Street, compliments of the department! Unfortunately, Big Al some how slipped through our hands. Nevertheless, he car jacked a car upon his get away, and thanks to 'Low Jack', we was able to locate him. But he wasn't in no condition to talk to us." And Detective Smith started laughing.

"What does this have to do with us?" Teyona asked.

"Let's just say that we are grateful that you two loved your father so much! Its strange how someone that you least expect, some how, turns out to be a blessing in disguise."

"We don't know what you're talking about!" Teyona emphasized.

"Sure you don't – how do you think that I knew that you were here. Please don't insult my intelligence! I've been a homicide detective for over 20 years, and this case was by far, the best that I ever worked. You did us a favor and we want you to know that we respect your efforts, and applaud your success. Listen, the department will offer your attorney 500 thousand a piece for your little law suit…take it and consider it a token of our appreciation! And also, you will be removed from my investigation, but if you deny to except our offer, then you will truly regret that decision!

However, I know that you two ladies are very smart, so I'm sure that we got a strong understanding! I wish you two the best of luck, and do take care of yourself." The detective said as he departed.

"Tey, Tey, it's time to roll! Bye, bye, daddy and Lala love you and rest in peace!

"Bye Daddy, Bye Lala, sleep with the angels! And don't worry about Grandma, we're going to take car of her, we promise! Love you Daddy! Kiss, kiss!"

The End

Look for **G. Prince** latest New Releases in Book Stores
and for purchase on **www.Amazon.com**

Ghetto Theory Publishing

Presents

The coldest West Coast tail every told.

Ghetto Games

Ghetto Games II, "the saga continues."

Ghetto Games III "Deadliest games ever played"

Natural Born Gangster

Am I My Sister's Keeper?

Rules of the Street Game that Every Hustler Should Know...!

Ghetto Games 1 & 2,
they are the hottest urban faction tales written and a
must read for anyone who enjoys the mind twisting
drama of the ghetto street life and passion that feed our
ambitions to struggle against all odds.

Ghetto Games II **"*The Ghetto Saga Continues*"**

This is the coldest and realest west coast
gangster street classic that has ever been written.
"If you like that west coast gangsta street shit…
then you will love this!
*Now available in paperback on Amazon.com &
Ghetto Theory.com*

Money, sex, murder, betrayal, drugs, and revenge
only spells one thing,
"Natural Born Gangster"

The Rules Of the Street
Game That Every
Hustler Should Know..!

G. PRINCE

This book is written and dedicated to all of the young hustlers, gangsta's, and players who choose to participate in the ghetto game. Because what you don't know can surely kill you, therefore, it's about time to set the rules straight!

www.ingramcontent.com/pod-product-compliance
Lightning Source LLC
Chambersburg PA
CBHW070625130626
46556CB00001B/476